T0354691

Brian Miller:
Joan of Arc & Danillia,
Terran Destroyer

Brian Miller:
Joan of Arc & Danillia, Terran Destroyer

(Full Throated) A non-Novella

Book Ten

J. MICHAEL BROWER

iUniverse

BRIAN MILLER: JOAN OF ARC & DANILLIA, TERRAN DESTROYER (FULL THROATED) A NON-NOVELLA

iUniverse books may be ordered through booksellers or by contacting:

iUniverse
1663 Liberty Drive
Bloomington, IN 47403
www.iuniverse.com
844-349-9409

ISBN: 978-1-6632-6714-6 (sc)
ISBN: 978-1-6632-6715-3 (e)

Library of Congress Control Number: 2024920054

Print information available on the last page.

iUniverse rev. date: 09/23/2024

Acknowledgement

For John Michael Atnip
and Bruce Alexander

—Hold off the earth awhile,
Till I have caught her once more in mine arms.
  [Leaps in the grave]

Now pile your dust upon the quick and dead,
  Till, of this flat, a mountain you have made
  T' o'ertop old Pelion or the skyish head
  Of blue Olympus.
—Laertes to departed Ophelia, *Hamlet*. Thanks to the
Folger Shakespeare Library

Research (and much, much respect) for The Donner Party, narrated by David McCullough (1933-2022), and The Dyatlov Pass Incident, by Nick Crowley, very gratefully acknowledged. Thanks, too, to Folger Shakespeare Library. Of The 47 Ronin, I acknowledge the author Seika Mayama and his play produced in 1941. Grateful acknowledgment also goes to the songs and poems mentioned, especially Judy Collins, Judith, *The Moon is a Harsh Mistress*. War No More is probably in the top three of ALL the poems I've heard. However, I'm just, *just* a…simple man.

Contents

~~PART ONE~~

Known Terrifier in the
Middle Kingdom

See her how she flies
Golden sails across the sky
Close enough to touch
But careful if you try
Though she looks as warm as gold
The Moon's a harsh mistress
The Moon can be so cold.

—JUDY COLLINS, *JUDITH*

—Ah, "Where is everyone and any-alien"? You teenagers ask me, Danillia, just *little-that*? Oh, the things a star dragon must suffer. Alright, orangutans, squishy fools, I'll play along. The Fermi paradox, Drake equation and the Kardashev scale? Don't make me laugh, it's all Puff-'n'- Stuff, slapdash. <u>DNA</u> is determining all, my simian-sillies, don't you see, here in the afternoon sunshine touching the Everglades? And anywhere else? Machines, in those few systems retaining them in the vastness of space, all that's left, dummies. You squishy humans are at the cusp of destruction. One mistake, it's all over. With all your drugs, senex (or zanaz, or sanix or alprazolam, other names of counterfeit-shit), fentanyl, Adderall, alcohol, heroin, cocaine, hosts of others. And look what the dragon stars have done? Just look! MORE drugs—you think drinking "the gods" blood has <u>saved</u> you? It's destroying your minds, only in a 'good' way, a dragon way, something <u>we</u> approve of? Someone on drugs, say, the wine they gave to the soldiers in World War One, will launch a nuke. Oh, maybe not tonight, maybe *some other* night, one day, for sure. Then, where will your world be? Dark Ages Some-Bigly! Limited Nuclear War <u>won't be</u> limited, right? Thanks to SAB for that one! Why don't you make that slip-up? Because of us, the saurians *wishing* for thirty companions. Only these ("selected"?) teens stand in the way? A water-based pulley of scatting monkeys, I <u>pine</u> for human annihilation! Stupid pride and vanity, determining all. The planets I've 'attended,' they are all dead, only machines replace them. The corporeal life compatible of THOUGHT, any humanesque thought—is GOING to kill <u>all</u> who stupidly possess it. And you given teenagers? You'd favor to spooge on women every seven to eight seconds, the "secret" of your human reproductive power? Your clandestine sport for the average minge? *Pandorum*, that movie, that's for you? Questions, questions by these simian sillies! Yeah, I've a tendency to watch human movies, but don't tell anybody. Citizens just living on one planet can't see that: either letting teens get in charge or wondering 'where the aliens are,' right? Now, onward. Ah, good afternoon! It's all very simple, everyone. So let me, Danillia Starblue, in my dragonesque form, put it simply. I <u>volunteer</u> myself to go to Asia, China, specifically. Not shape-shifted, that's old hat. As a one-star-dragon-expeditionary-mission? Just before all companions and dragons leave this Earth. To reconnoiter the Middle Kingdom, as the Lord of the Lizardanians, Littorian, apparently, wishes? I'll make it a colorful visit, that's my watchword, I'll make it positively bloom. Everyone agrees to this—silence means compliance, right, Brian? And Mr. Miller, no one else, if the group pleases, to represent gentle humanity. Even though Brian's not my companion, don't worry your reptilian craniums there. I won't let him get all 'dragon' on us. I'll defend against his cultural appropriation. No chance on churning my yogurt into KY Jelly, okay my young, vigorous teenager? His "local wives" might like that, but I shan't. However, I'm willing to be this human's step-and-fetch it, ready to go, Brian?

Horrified, somewhat vilified at this sinister monologue, racist stuff was scandalous-alone, I was assured of a negative reaction among the dragon stars, all gathered around, *writ large*. I couldn't believe what I'd heard. So, I looked around, a self-satisfied smirk, my mask. No reason to say anything, right? Right? Shocking, what happen next!

—Sounds reasonable enough for me, right Clareina?

Clare blinked her massive eyes at Larascena.

—Agreeable to you, agreeable to me, too.

Matter concluded, draconianly, as all the dragon stars assembled just dismissed it, entire. My recent wives were going to let this happen? Larascena, the great Warlord of all Alligatoria, then Clareina, the young Lizardanian, stared at me, with a 'see-ya' gaze in those myriad (and utterly mysterious), super-wide eyes. And, thinking nothing, it was all over for them. They began casually looking at the sky, maybe in anticipation of leaving the Earth altogether.

Katrina gazed at me, shaking my arm vigorously.

—Brian Miller, doesn't Danillia hate you most of all? What's this zombie-talk from Clare and Lara? They don't care that you'll be at Danillia's mercy? They think you're going to be okay with her? Not to repeat history, but let's do: Didn't she want the Earth to get destroyed by the Twins of Triton, the twin meteors? Didn't she want Littorian to get strung up, at that ridiculous trial? Didn't she defeat Korillia on Lizardania and then Clare, too, and wanted to make a saurian shish kabob out of you? Didn't she also try to—

Danillia, agitated. The reptilian snapped her fingers over the delay in my summons like a shotgun blast busting any double-door-big-league. This saurian was not to be beclowned.

—Hey, hey! The Middle Kingdom awaits, Brian, come here. You deal with that double-dealing Russian later, let's go!

At the wonder of all the bagel-mouthed-companions Rachel Dreadnought and Jason Shireman just politely smiled. The leaders of my companion rivals, agreed with Danillia in a delightful way, and actually waived good-bye! Rachel blew me a kiss. It was as if Danillia had a love-affair with me. Jason turned away, knowing that wasn't true. Without another word, leaving all Black World weapons behind (it would be rude to bring those armaments on a supposed peace-mission) Danillia took me (and maybe Biblically, too).

On our flight, just when we left Florida, Danillia turned her massive equine-esque head around.

—You like flying with me? My little someone-else's companion? Oh, I don't give a country-care whether you're enjoying it or not. Breaking in on your companion-contentment, let's get down to business. I'm sure you knew this was coming.

Green, puissant scales rolled by, like I was greased in WD-40. Her vast pinions, upside down now, veined leathery wings, she looked majestic. Of a sudden, I felt an extreme grip on my hips. Dragon blood failing fast, I had to think rapidly, maybe even abstractly.

—My lady, if you crush my waist together, like I know you certainly can do, I won't be able to—

—Oh, the <u>hole</u> you're digging, and what? Listen for a notable, distinguished pop, coming on fast. As I squash your frame into an attractive hood ornament? Wait until my gorgeous muscles make your bones squeeze together like any over-ripe banana. Let's play a game. In about one minute I'll squish all the way through you like an over-ripe grape. Wouldn't that be fun?

—Your pouting abdominals are the material of gods, my lady.

—And your unctuousness is in question, too, right-when I'm about to end you. And once your nature-boy hips are destroyed, we'll get to the business-side of that Evergreen question of the 'rest' of you. I've got a total of ten feet of rock-hard muscle. I mean, just feel those Everest peaks, away up on-my-mightiness! I was stunned with the power sliding off those giantess biceps. I obligatorily caressed them.

—Wow, they're ultra-hard, my mightiness.

—That's without magic, too, almost sixty-inches across these Cyclopean gigantisms, which will make these human 'hipsters' into solid-bone-cracking-jelly. How many human lifetimes I spent growing my arms, I couldn't tell. Oh, I know, I know. Admittedly, you have dragon blood from Larascena, Clareina, and Littorian, right? Maybe more saurians, you're so blessed, Brian. What can't be cured must be endured, but not for long. Thing is, I'm old, very, very old. I have spells for this trip you'll know well. Am I skipping ahead? Not that you could help squealing in your piggy-voice. I'm squishing you like an accordion, crushing right through those star dragon layers of shields running around your bones? Nice resistance, but it's no match for me. How does a guy get so squirted and Kah-Smashed into my dominant arms? How did you get so hopelessly pinched by my angelic seven-inch claws? Human, you reached much too high, and, in the past, I've been wronged too much by little you. Answer to the question 'why'? My demolishing begins with a spell I've 'hatched' over all the saurians on your 'left side of the bus,' dummy! Don't worry, they'll realize my spell. Realization too late.

I knew I was in the deepest-dragon-borne-trouble. For the tenth time, I couldn't believe <u>my own saurians</u> could be so deceived. They should be watching for a spell from this dragon star. Danillia was, and is, so powerful. Chances <u>were</u>, she'd numerous spells saved up for this event.

—Chances <u>*are*</u>, silly human! Chances <u>are</u>! You think straight, pigmy, I'm monitoring you.

I did have my mental defenses up, but up against Danillia? She'd invaded some of my thoughts, too. Maybe she couldn't follow along completely? I had to take a risk on that. The dragon star was a daughter of God? Definitely of a <u>fallen</u> god.

—Danillia, I have to say your muscles are feminine and structurally ginormous, too.

—Dispense with your obsequiousness when life's dangerously close to ending. Your mind's blown-in a bit now, eh? Vitals, when at attention, constitute a form of muscle, right, Brian? At some point, you must get more strategic with your (dragon-star-induced) apparatus. Oh, I know your old human debate, is it a muscle or an organ? Magnificent, Olympian phallus? Guess what? I've a mega-muscle, too, and can griddle that mega-lance down to mere mush-and-slush. Even if it reaches three feet, enticed with its veiny goodness, as my two un-favorite saurians like? <u>Unlike</u> Clare and Lara, you'll not violate me. If you just do, there on my back, I'll squeeze, shift-snuff and eviscerate that brawny shaft into mincemeat, to sludge, with my virginial galaxy-box. It will be mega-death of your meat-hammer, grinding your mighty bazooka into a soft, moist paste. Like the sound of that? Some of your people, our pets, sure do. Your "favorite" muscle ground-dog-down to nothing but gunk-goo? I'm getting dragon-star-moist just thinking about destroying your shifty-shaft. Mashing, mushing, rutting and ploughing your miserably weak body, Lilith-on-top, right? I'll turn your proud Puff-the-One-Eyed-Dragon into a spineless slush, like ten-day-gone-yogurt, dripping to the floor? I will close my viral muscle completely around your muzzle-angler, obliterating that trembling invader, until you are literally mega-priss-throttled. I'll mortify your pride, oh, yes. Then I'll eunuchize you; ripping all your blood-soaked-bowling-ball-sized-gonads up and out with my unyielding, saurian-superwoman-ripping-claws. Ken-Doll-Here-You-Cum, right? My strength, just overwhelming. Can't you just see my shiny teeth chumping on those veiny-jewels for my *Elevenses*, wanna-be Clydesdale?

I swallowed, gamely enough, at this sinister and supremely scatological monologue. I *wanted* to say I'm not going to get with this reptilian stinky skank under any conditions. Thought better of it. I put a 'mental shell' on all non-obsequious thoughts: I'd be her groveling toady today.

—And then, alas! I can't tell you of The Donner Party, a shame it'd be if you missed out on that, my Eminence!

The crushing-squeezing was stilled, the dragon star, wide-eyed. She was curious, wanted to know. Obviously, you must be pleasant, and be a good storyteller. Not a great one—'good tales' are enough.

—The Donner Party? What's that, speak, bottom-feeder!

I went on pleadingly, if not with any pleasantry.

—Just a story, but oh, what a story it is, too bad you'll miss.

—Stupid street cleaner of the human shit-conscience, maybe I'll get a goat to lick your vitals, right? Now doff your hat, we're leaving Florida, at 5,000 feet up? I'm just thinking about licking your selected dragon minges, don't mind me. What god would goddamn want you to 'transcend' anywhere? You vile creature, as I'll show you, anon. Now we are flying over Mississippi. I've slowed down this dragon-flight, I don't want to miss this, my near-to-death human! Good that you have an atmosphere, an 'environment,' that I'm providing, but I need to hear your servile voice.

Oh, I just need to know this story, I'm just strangely frenzied about it. I see you've protected your mind; I could get the memory out by ripping it from your brain. You've drunk (or drank?) dragon-star blood, and a lot of it, too. I will listen. If you have a good story, violently adventurous?

—Danillia my story is just the greatest event of human suffering that you could imagine, my regal lady, taking place out West. And it's not just the greatest event of human anguish, it's distress in general of all kinds, even a dragon would want to know, can you relax your mighty grip so I can tell it, my lady? But it's okay to finish me, I—

—Let me hear <u>first</u> of the Donner Party, speak Brian and I might let you survive a little longer, only in order to tell me. So speak!

—My lady, so please you. In the 1840s, folks needed to get to California so—

—California? Oh, that's one of your nuisance states, I guess? It doesn't matter from up here in the air, states are just an artificial construction. I can identify them, because, well, I'm a dragon star, duh! We'll fly over California soon, just give me the location?

—I've seen maps, I can't give you just where it is, my lady so—

—It's something to go on, think it to me, maggot-minion?

I cringed at that abysmal reference (she had a habit of that), but I dutifully obeyed the dragon star. I didn't want to rub her scales the wrong way unless surrounded by saurian friends. At this point, I had no friends, at least, near me. Flying with her, a harsh mistress, tell a good story, or <u>splat</u>, overfilled trash bag would be my end (with squashed hips).

—Hmmm, what's this, thought defenses up? I could penetrate those notions, even if they are saurian based. You've no real experience with a mind as old as mine.

—That'd give me a headache, interfering with my story, so—

—Oh, alright, tell on. Tell, tell!

—At this time, 1846 was the worst winter on record, my Esteemed lady. Only 20,000 or so immigrants lived west of the Mississippi River.

Then it developed into a human-flood, as more people wanted to move West, for various reasons. High in the Sierra-Nevada, there was the tale of the sad Donner Party. Ambition, greed, stupid failures, and, all-the-while, wanting to take a short-cut. In 1845, an author wanted to get more folks to go West. That writer was Lansford W. Hastings. So he wrote the Immigrants Guide to Oregon and California, wishing people to move West.

—Why's that, my human? Be quick!

—Financial panic, outbreaks of sickness and that insatiable need for Manifest Destiny, to move West. For instance, the Mormons moved to Utah with Brigham Young—

—Alright, go on, speed it up!

—Yes, my Empress. Hastings had never really seen the route he thought would be best. For some, the American Dream was a tragedy of the worst kind. In April 1846, a bunch of wagons started out from Springfield, Illinois, George and Jacob Donner and James Reed, took their families West. Reed was leading the group at first, but he acted like royalty, you see. Doesn't that sound familiar? Oops, strike that. They had a big wagon with a stove, cots for sleeping, spring-cushioned seats, the Pioneer Palace Car. It was an elaborate affair too, my Eminence. Independence, Missouri was where they were headed to get into that 'long wagon train,' going to California and Oregon. They had to go next to Indian Territory, so that—

—You mean Native Americans, right? Now you've got 'immigrants' moving from Haiti taking advantage of this societal shoplifting? Capitalism rutting on the poor, damn humans are trash.

—Well, uh, they were called 'Indians' because the original discoverers, from Portugal or Spain, were on their way to India, and just never changed it back, I guess. That's an example of a sobriquet, my lady.

—What fruit-loops those explores were; just go on.

—Ah, sure, my Queenly. It was a journey full of perils, and, did you know, about 50% of the people on the Donner Party were under 18? It was an epic and epical, that's for sure, 2,500 miles until they could get to Sutter's Fort, in California. They couldn't pass over such a distance like a winged saurian can. Wind-swept plains, three or four mountain ranges, half a dozen scorching deserts, and time was everything. They had to get over the Sierra-Nevada mountains before snow came. Hasting's Cutoff assured them they'd make it. His pamphlet tantalized the Donners and the Reeds. They thought they could go over the Wasatch Mountains, under the Great Salt Lake, through the desert and the Rubies, into California. They started out in the company of 7,000 wagons, at least that's what Tamsen Donner said. The wagons started on May 12th. However, the Mexican American War of 1846 was just beginning, and everyone was going to that—maybe, at some point, I'll tell you of the story of the Alamo, but that was 1836. Anyhow, they got to the Big Blue River—

—Yup, and there it is, Kansas, see my simian?

—Oh, yes, my Sovereign. I'd prefer it if you don't refer to me as—

—And you're in no position to make preferences, scat-monkey. Go on with the story before I turn you inside out. Don't think I can't: I'll drive my hand into your mouth and pull you out by the ass-sphincter. Isn't it great to be with a star dragon *wanting* to eat your backside?

I swallowed a sickly stick of massive cancer.

—The Pioneer Palace Car was a labor to them. Margaret Reed's mother was the first casualty. She died of consumption.

—What's that, quickly?

—It's TB.

—You and your abbreviations. I'll kill you for that, just not right now. What's TB?

—Tuberculosis. My lady.

—And that is?

—Plague, an obscenity, it'll kill you.

—You mean it will kill <u>you</u>, simple mandrill!

—Not me, your highness, at least, not now.

—Oh, yes, of course, of course. The Tree of Life, <u>bestial</u> that it's in you. No real matter. I'll have my revenge on certain dragons for that one. You can still die by violence, but I'm getting ahead of myself. Go on!

—On June 27th, my saurian pre-Eminence, they reached Fort Laramie. They were only a week behind schedule. At this point, an old friend they saw at the fort tried to convince Mr. Reed to follow the regular route. He was sure wagons couldn't go over Hasting's Cutoff. Just the need to take a short-cut in life, we are all going to die one day, so—

—That is, you are, obsidian-ape-teenager.

Danillia's knowing glance, as she shifted a massive eye back and up to me, with a self-same serpentine smile.

—You must go for it, sometimes. If your human, you have to. Reed was a good guy, reasonable. You have to take a short-cut, if you're sure of it. Reed was sure of it. So, on July 20th, they reached the Little Sandy River. Most people chose right, but the Donner's selected the left road. They elected a captain, and Reed's imperial ways and wealth didn't impress. They selected George Donner. Just another mistake in democracy, right there, my Danillia. A week later, they rolled into Fort Bridger, with Jim Bridger running it like a trading-post. Mr. Hastings, the author they were effectively following, wasn't there, he'd went on ahead, with other wagons, saying any other immigrants could follow behind. Hastings Cut-Off was a saving of 350 or 400 miles. According to Mr. Hastings, that is. But Mr. Bridger said it was a good way to go. Captain Sutter's Fort was only 700 miles away, seven weeks, so said James Reed. But they were stimmed—

—What the hell does that crappy word mean? You alphabet-mafia-Zulu, it doesn't translate to *Universalian* at all, talk in plain language or I'll throttle you, raggedy-chimp!

I was 5,000 feet up on a hostile dragon star, I had to watch myself.

—Sorry, my lady: That means they came to a halt. It really means 'self-stimulating behavior' and maybe I'm using it wrong, my heartfelt apologies. Continuing now, my lady: The road ahead was not good. It was already early in August. They stopped at Echo Canyon in Utah and—

—You mean right there, maggoty-ass-chimpanzee?

This saurian had the vision of a three-or-four times eagle and the GPS of a, well, a dragon!

—Yes, lady, there. Wow, you are making progress to the Middle Kingdom, a place I'd like to see, so please you, my Queen. Hastings, in a written note they found on the road, said to stay there and look for a better way. James Reed went to find him. Hastings was reluctant to lead the immigrants and so Reed had to do the job of leading people up Big Mountain. Then they reached the shore of the Great Salt Lake, it'd taken longer than they thought. On August 27th, the 87 immigrants had 600 miles to go. West and then south. Summer was going fast. They had to cross the desert, the Salt Desert. It was August 30th. The oxen bolted, when they went across, and it was a disaster. Five days to cross the desert, 36 oxen where lost, and the Pioneer Palace Car was abandoned.

—Damn. They are having a hard time of it.

This was the first sign of sympathy and I longed to hear this. Then she followed with this zinger.

—…right, you mega-yard-ape?

—Very hard time, my highness. They could not get back to Fort Bridger. Inventory of provisions was drawn up. They didn't have enough to make it to California. On September 27th they reached the Humboldt River, in Nevada, where the trail met up with the established one. Could they make it before the snow fell? The race was on. The Cut-Off was 125 miles longer and most-everything was lost going through it, including a lot of animals, cattle. On October 5th, Reed got in real trouble.

—What happened, by the gods? Say it, you orangutan, or I'm going to smash your behind from inside your mouth! And don't think I <u>can't</u> do it, either. Let me interrupt you with this little thought. Isn't the conditioning of Artificial Intelligence the end of humanity? Nuclear war looms, just as the Military-Industrial complex desires. It will be by accident, not intentional, we Dragon Stars have our companions and just want to go, the hell with human affairs. You, Brian Miller, keep thinking of <u>excuses</u> causing us to stay, causing <u>me</u> to disobey. I want to go; you keep me here. So, I've got to entertain myself, the dragon-borne way. I'll show you where your excuses can take you, anon!

I forced myself to go on. Backtalk here, a huge splat down on the rocks below. Or some kinda unknown ass-whipping, myself as the dragons' meat (on a hammer).

—My lady, if I can go on with my story? He killed somebody (like I'd like to do). Reed was arguing with this guy as he whipped his oxen. The fellow turned right-around and started flogging Reed with his whip. Reed got his hunting knife and killed this dude. People were interested in hanging but settled on exile. Reed rode out of camp, banished, and his family cried endlessly. I guess the 'democratic' decision was made, maybe we can chat about that but not right now. The Donner party traveled on. The immigrants knew they were coming apart. On October 12th, Piute Indians killed a portion of oxen with poisoned arrows. Now they were down below 100 head of cattle. They reached the Truckee Lake. On October 19th, food was nearly gone—they were desperate.

At this point, an actual shiver made itself felt on me. Maybe it was from the dragon star? A chance-thought occurred. We are getting somewhere, I knew she couldn't be that cruel, maybe she is coming around to sympathize with these pioneers, you are doing right with this story, I just knew it!

—Then good news—the men they'd sent on to Sutter's Fort returned with seven mules loaded with food. They were going to make it after all!

—Geez, I thought there was something to this story, good that they are going to make it over that last peak. 'Course, I could grab a big piece of land and then fly them over the mountain. Or just turn into an attractive

Godzilla and step over that facial scab, sprinkling the Donner's down at Fort Sutter!

—It didn't work out that way, my lady, because they rested at Truckee Lake for five days—and then, winter storms took over. Thing is, they shouldn't have waited so long. Before that, the Donner's wagon wheel broke and George Donner cut his hand, trying to fix it. That delayed the party further. George's hand turned into gangrene. Meantime, the way out was blocked by snow. The blizzard did its job, and the pass out of Truckee Lake was completely blocked. They'd lost time by literally a day or two, to get over the pass, so they had to build a winter camp. And it snowed, and snowed and yes, you guessed it. The folks at Sutter's Fort, had to save the immigrants. Reed was in charge of relief parties, he'd made it through to California. But he could get no men to do it; they were all off fighting the Mexicans. The people tried to get out. They couldn't. The 81 members of the Donner Party consisted of 25 men, 15 women, and 41 children in two winter camps. And all that you do, Danillia, can't compare with starvation. And then what follows is...

—Is what, my little baboon?

—It's cannibalism, my lady.

The saurian was silent.

—So? On with it!

—So, say that <u>word</u>, my highness, then, I'll go on.

The reptilian looked around, surprised. In pleasant flight, with an atmosphere around me, she <u>had</u> to say it.

—Okay my temporarily privileged human. <u>Please</u>?

—Alright my Queenly Prominence. Most of the cattle were killed, the Donners had to stay until next Spring. The people were miserable, all starving. Thanksgiving came. The snow, about three-feet-deep. It continued to accumulate, foot-on-foot. All cattle killed and consumed. Bark, leaves, old bones, anything to eat during these dark days. On December 16th, the strongest ones, called themselves "The Forlorn Hope," tried to escape. Snow blindness hit the selected settlers as they walked high in the California Mountains, hopelessly lost. Cannibalism soon took over the "Hope." God was asked to help. He...wasn't available. A pioneer died, and then another and another. One Patrick Dolan cut the meat off the dead. The awful food invigorated them, so they struggled on. The two Indians, from Sutter's Fort, were killed, then eaten. At Truckee Lake, people were dying left and right. Someone *had* to help these people: Relief parties were sent. Assistance had to come. James Reed led the second relief party. The first party was on its way. Meanwhile, people were buried in the snow, with blankets over them. That is, those who weren't on the plate for others to eat. On February 19th, the first relief party was on the frozen Truckee Lake. No one was there. Then, a woman emerged from a hole in the snow. "Are you men from California...or do you come from Heaven?" The relief party could only take 24 of the people out. Then, on February 26th—

—Hey, why didn't some humans fish at the lake?

—What?

—Manners, mind, beast-of-the-field. Ah, never-you-mind. Why didn't they fish, you wanna-be-reptile?

—Well, you're right, my regent. Uh, I don't know, maybe they did, and it was unsuccessful, my lady. It's a good question.

—Go on, soiled-diapers-man-ape?

That really grated on me. However, I knew the destructive power of the beast, me trying to subtly correct this sickening set of pejoratives.

—The Donner Party's troubles were far from over. Four more relief parties struggled to get the Donner Party from the high snow. The scenes enacted in those months can never be forgotten. Mothers before dissolving children, the men no food to bring home. When the first relief party reached the Lake, Patty Reed, then eight years old, wanted to stay behind to care for her brother, Thomas. "Well, ma, if you never see me again, do the best that you can." Then the second relief party came to help the first. James Reed was leading it. Margaret Reed hadn't seen James in all that time, five months. At the Lake, it was all chaos. People went crazy, just crazy. Maybe you'd know what that's like? Demons, not humans, lingered at the Truckee, and even the Native Americans avoided the immigrants when they witnessed cannibalism. George Donner and Tamsin Donner were inseparable. They died and were cannibalized. It was all a horror show. The fourth relief party was delayed by a month. On April 21st, the fourth relief team left the lake and on April 25th, they reached Bear Valley. All of the survivors had come out of the mountains. It could have been avoided if people hadn't gone for a 'short-cut'. That's how it was for the Russian Revolution, too. Lenin and Trotsky wanted all the Russians to 'jump ahead,' to defy their DNA, live socialism and communism. Thing was: The peasants; just 'little' bourgeoisie waiting-to-happen. It wasn't to be, and they got Stalin, instead. Millions died as a result. I think the <u>clothes</u> people wore, the uniforms, de-humanized people, let them kill their fellow creatures. Well, that's all I've to say on this. People keep making different choices, but all the mistakes are repeated (over and over). Maybe that could change on different worlds, like in the Goldilocks Zone or the Butterfly Zone, this, the Donner Party and the Russian Revolution was the Twilight Zone. For me, I've tried to 'get ahead' and have dragons here to lead us all to a better life. I think my time with you will be that result and that's what I get, trying, sincerely, to make things better. I've made them worse, that is, this flight with you. Humans can be animals and you're comparing me with lower forms of life, isn't really wrong. We <u>are</u> animals. For the Donner Party, 87 people started out. 46 survived. 41 died. 5 women, 14 children and 22 men, dead. Two-thirds of the men buried (if not cannibalized). The family of the Donners suffered most. Now, the Donner Camp is a tourist attraction. A real shame, and only a true-teenager can tell this story sincerely to a saurian. People are fragile, please know that if nothing else. The thing we have is love, the Reed's love shown in the Sierra-Nevada mountains when James found some of his family, two children still remained at Truckee Lake. I will tell you this, my noble reptilian, as a reminder to all: "Remember, never take no cut-offs and hurry along as fast as you can." That's from Virginia Reed. When the human race, when people like Virginia stop fighting against the odds, against the frigid cold—and even fighting a crazy saurian like you—that's when we lose our humanity. And that's a good place to end such a story, my lady.

When the Donner story was over, I reacted with a smidgen of hope over the malicious intentions of Danillia. The saurian was indeed hesitant. At least, I thought.

—Wow, that was a good story. Your execution is temporarily halted, the Pacific Ocean is just there. I do like your spark, Brian. You are notoriously misdirected, though. Can you see the ocean, from here? Maybe only I can. I've an idea, let's play a little game. Back to the scene of the crime? Ah, this is just the time for it.

I was confused, but that didn't matter to Danillia. The winged saurian warped down to the Nevada-California mountains, arriving at this sign:

Donner Camp
PICNIC GROUND
Historical Site
Tahoe National Forest

—See how 'picnic ground' is in larger letters? That's wormwood for me. Just let me at those 'tourons,' if we should find any. Bad day for them if we do. And stop your confounded, faux-melancholic face, Brian, or I'll squish it off. And you know I can. So, Brian. Know what I've been doing, of late?

—No, my Empress, please inform me?

—Why, killing humans, of course! What do you think Jason Shireman was up to, just my arm-candy?

I was in profound shock.

—Ah, your legs are shaking. Don't shake too much, someone will get ideas, you little two (or three?) timer. I'll keep you from smashing yourself in the vitals, believe me.

With an iron will, I relaxed my legs.

—A selection of your people have written in, or contacted me on Twitter (or X?), Facebook, Snapchat, TikTok, all that social media stuff, asking me, <u>particularly</u> me, Danillia, to end them. Must have heard (or read) of my superpowers-superpower over every other dragon star, this happens anywhere I go. Everything and anything is just hook-ups and contacts, anyway! Jason coordinated it all, as a good companion should.

—Is that so, my lady?

At first, I didn't believe her.

—Don't frenchtoast me. Anyone and everyone would be graced to have a god like *moi* finish them, end them. Hell, had to do something when you delayed dragon stars all that time? Jason Shireman understood. He even endorsed it. Oh, I admit, most are sick and old or just 'sick' literally. I've had 54 humans, so far. Some quickly, some longer. I'm very good with human bodies, too. Most are men. They are tired of this life and want, need, a dragon to obliterate them utterly. Star dragons are an imposing 'ender' don't you think? And there have been a few young ones. I've had a few women, too, very young females, the kind wanting to die in my powerful claws. And a treat to me, some were pregnant! Hideous you say? Know why? Because they couldn't take their givens in this world. A couple of examples: A middle-aged man at 58? I destroyed that one, proud to do so. Dragons have to make sacrifices for our pets. First, I allowed him his jollies, you know, lifting him up and down, grabbing his vitals and jerking him to tender explosion, just stuff like that. Men are all about sex and power, they have no other redoubt! They love woman-muscle, I guess. Then, repeatedly and rapidly bored, I ripped an electric shock to his face, knocking his eyes out, which hung there just like red and white cords, mini-belt hooks. That was fascinating to me, for about eight seconds, then human-driven-generation-Z-boredom-kicked-in. Can't blame a dragon for getting with the native populace, now can you? The gods, I've been around humans too long. So, he started screaming, lickspittle fool. I zipped his mouth closed, I've a spell for that. Nuisance screaming indeed. I admit, being a Lizardanian, I'm not 'magically made,' not like an Alligatorian. Crocs have fire, so hot no human can imagine it, that's their gift. The Wysterians, well, they know magic and everything dragon associated. Me? I hate, *can't stand*, human screaming. Then I stripped him buck-naked, ripped his nails off (all 20 of them), broke his arms, legs and femur, burned his genitals off, put my claws through his intestines, stirring them up like so much crimson lasagna, shattered a glass and forced it down his throat, then I burned him entire without impacting the nerves, a very skilled thing, requiring a real intimacy with human bodies. Then I just finished him with a little dragon magic—trigeminal neuralgia lasting as long as I felt. I didn't let him go unconscious, disallowing those painkillers like endorphins and serotonins and stuff. Oh, no. I wasn't giving him anything, inflicting the worst pain I could produce. I pride myself on the level of suffering I can cause. Had guys that wanted their skulls crushed to the *point* of passing out. More like 'passing on' as I blew brains to the ceiling with my muscular legs. For the rest, I just went through my medical book on all the worse agonies you humans can feel. Then—

—My goodly lady, I think I've heard enough.

—I'll decide what is enough, simian-silly. Roasting women in a bronze bull is perhaps my favorite torture. Did that on one grimy, foul, raggedy young bitch. Made her nose into a bone-crushed-triangle, too. Then, I smashed her brain-in, so slowly, with my left hand, called it my "Neurocranium Crush," wish you'd seen it. With that move, I'm able to force the brain out of her mouth. And the tongue goes first, see? I've distended her jaw, Cobra-like, easy work for *moi*. Yes, I do magic with some victims: Numerous stonefish stings, gallstones, tetanus, rusty nails inserted just anywhere, multiple appendix bursts, intense gout, flaying skin, dislocations (I'm very good at that!), massive kidney stones that are just intolerable (for my men, mainly, like giving birth times 100), testicular torsion cord twists, and slow-motion-ripping of bones is my excruciating thing to do with these God-(god?)-given claws. And, my child, I'm going to do the same to you!

The star dragon marshalled her brutal fists together, cracking them mightily, a truly unfathomable force. And sure enough, at Truckee Lake, around the Donner's camp, five families were touring. I took a little risk.

Run, run, run!

The reptilian was positively giggling at the tourists nosing-around. Then she reacted to my contemplation, alert as any thought-Tom-cat.

Don't, sucker! I'll spread and slit your buttocks open like a <u>*sea bass*</u> *in front of all these tourons? Better pucker up, don't want any of those innards displayed? That fillet is* <u>*easy*</u> *for those* <u>*who know*</u>*. My 'environment' will just direct your notions to me, anyway, so sit by your goddamn dish. See, human, even your thoughts are known to me. Neither your body nor your feelings can escape my saurian clutches. Clutches! Oh, I enjoyed that final word, love to say it, good that you've given me an incident to 'wrap it' around. Like the pun? Oh, let me enjoy!*

I discontinued thinking in their direction immediately. I was completely downcast, because this dragon was certifiably crazy. Danillia needed a mad house, definitely so. I'd never would go with her, *knowing* the extent of her sinister phantasms.

Every/anything the dragon did, in her own mind, was justified.

She wasn't sympathetic or concerned in the least for humankind. The saurian was like any human world-leader: hungry for individual ambition, to make world-history <u>her</u> way. Anyone getting in the way, would just have to be eliminated. That did not include selected humans, Danillia's companion for instance, and a few, fortunate others. The Lizardanian had the magic-power, inducing the world-over, to get what she wanted. That, no matter what.

The dragon star landed with a vigorous flourish, melting her wings inside herself. I, her faux companion, hopped off. The drop was four or five feet, but I was used to it, dragon-blood notwithstanding.

She gathered the group together, like a Pied- Piper-of-Ham-Bloody-Burglar-Hill. All five families came together, crowding around her, all with admiration for the great beast. The dragon star smiled sweetly, not revealing any sign of her myriad teeth. The reptilian waved her hands at them, even hugging the parents, making them feel at ease. The elders just dismissed me. She nodded at her extreme bulk, bulwarking strongly for each and every tourist, feeding their eyes like a Donner Camp victim of famine. Of course, mesmerism took them all. I forgave them of at least that. First time in front of a dragon (star)? No doubt. And no one even thought to signal anyone with cellphones, or some such. Why would they when Danillia's subtle manipulation washed over the tourists-complete? Didn't they want a 'selfie' with the dragon? Even that was tertiary in their thoughts. A shame and a sham notion, Danillia's magic would prevent any phones from operating, anyway. That might interfere with any ghoulishness, which would follow, anon.

Danillia lifted, with both mini-Godzilla hands, picking up two gigantic boulders with ease, these weighing in excess of twenty tons. These rocks tightened her body, as was her wont. I was accustomed to such power-displays. Still, all the tourists whispered at this, like teetering to a Wilhelm scream. She nestled down, amazing tail making a scaled ring, that the children could climb up. She rocked the giant boulders, in slow motion, up and down for hungry, venerating eyes to see. Yes, and sit they did, tantalized at fondling the saurians' massive, stunningly oblique sinews. I, mouth parted, stood back, almost forced back. I was part of her scheme, too.

With her great reptilian head, she had the kids come up and literally caress her Cyclopean biceps, puckered to prove. With magical entreaty, Danillia made the peaks stand at ridged attention, sculpted, way-up-on-majesty. Frankly, I'd never seen such a pouting structure on any saurian woman's arms, reaching Everest heights. The youths, thinking they were in heaven and an angel was sat before them, they reached up, willingly, fondling the vastness of the saurian's mighty guns. With the adolescents, all thrown around into a make-shift corral of her tail, the parents hung off to the left, albeit, joyfully entertained. To emulate the children, feeling-away at this colossal creature's body, affected (and positively infected) the parents in the most peculiar way. Power and sex mixed together in this magnificent bowl of *commanding* ultra-life.

Tremors of delight and enchantment ran through all eight children. They were dazzled, properly aligned on Danillia's sinuous tail. Maybe she had a spell on them. Probably she didn't.

So right up under the sign, SITE OF THE BREEN CAMP, Donner Party, 1846-7, the saurian acted out. And what a horrendous performance, suitable for a saurian-at-war-with-all-humankind (only, these humans didn't know it).

Nevertheless-and-all-the-more, the children cossetted, caressed and playfully touched the dragon star's cobble-stone-abs, giggling. They wondered at the tremors spouting and sprouting-out of those impressive scales, making Danillia's mega-ton-obliques into rippling, planks of green, strengthened steel.

—Yes, I'll abase myself so you can get both hands around my peaks on this ginormous bicep. Come, come, get your kiddy-passions out. Those boulders are a minuscule twenty tons apiece, appropriate enough for you? I knew you human kiddies would like this little strength display. You five boys, goodness what's going on in your loins, right? Your, what, 11 or 12 years old? Bulging out entirely, eh? Three girls and five boys? My lassies getting a little squishy? That's pleasant as all get-out. Think of me as your all-gender slave, I'll do whatever you wish, and that, immediately?

Not following exactly, the children when along with the dragon-hymn of Danillia, rejoicing. If you weren't used to the magic of her forked tongue, however, as I certainly was. At this point, Danillia was on the verge of orgiastic victory over her new-found-minions. For this reptilian, 'talking dirty' was all matter-of-course. Cuddling and encouraging them on her massive, ponderous tail. That elongated structure Danillia held still. Like rats on random meat, they singularly and collectively "felt the reptilian up" into crowning majesty, she bending obediently down.

This is what humans, even young ones, must do for a dragon, oh, the shear gullibility of it all, Brian. Be completely mystified, by me and mine. What a terrifier I'm going to give them, and you, Brian Miller Human, like John in Revelation, here to see all!

The terrific things, the mass-Hobbesian-horrorfests this creature did to the eight innocent broods, no one has any words for. It was unbelievable, ineffable, unnamable, unimageable. I won't go all-H.P. Lovecraft on you, I've an obligation to describe, at least some of it, the rest, Upchuck Metropolis, choking to death on my own sick.

Of a sudden, Danillia brought the two massive rocks together, tons and tons of raw-unexpurgated-muscle-power. Spitting and splitting through flesh and bones, right on the upper-bodies and heads, of all the unknowing kids. A sheen of blood spouted from each of them; two eyes, four, no six, arrived at my feet, dancing around like coins at any Penny Arcade machine. The horrible, surprised orbs looked up at me.

Snake eyes?

Maybe a spell caused by Danillia.

Probably that. Their faces were splatted on the 'environment,' around me, filaments and fragments of a once-human design. At least the atmosphere was still up, but it had all the kid's skin sliding and slipping down like oiled film on a rainy day. Those observers had astonishment and fear build into their very flesh with the combined, reddened offal. My eyes, windshield wipers, crying. The 'environment' acting like a cerise window of absolute horror, the children looking more like bloody insect-window-splats on a speeding car.

—You remember when a known-alien said, 'you are the monster here'? I've seen it wandering around in your thoughts like a pinball. Now, it's me, <u>me</u>, ME, I'm the monster, and *little you*? Just my lickspittle. Isn't that better <u>than</u> minion, you pre-food?

A miscellaneous child was spilt slowly open in the serpents' mean-mega-hands. For the other children, it ended quite hastily. Two others, it was minutes to the end, but what insane minutes!

Danillia ruined all of them, but that wasn't the end of their trouble at her sudden arrival. Death be not proud? The star dragon would make it <u>proud</u>, the red delights and multiple sorrows, the ultra-demise-dealer.

At-the-sudden, chaos-and-dispensed cruelty unbound, Danillia laughed (and thought) down to me.

—You like this? This was mere foreplay! I've the godlike strength to perform boiling, keelhauling, Catherine wheels, extracting brains with crushing hand power, pear(s) of anguish (with my claws alone, I can stretch out anyone's mouth or down-backside-south), Diogenes' Pants, Judas Cradles, Blood Eagles and a speeded-up version of Scaphism. Of the last latter, it just takes too long; 17 days? I'll make it 24 (fun) hours.

The saurian turned to the frightened adults.

—Given I've something planned for Brian, we'll just have to go with something quick for you guys, right?

Only one woman was pregnant. I lamented it (so fully), praying Danillia wouldn't notice her. Danillia suddenly turned to me and smiled all those seven-inch teeth.

—Let's have some fun—heard of Roe vs. Wade?

The dragon turned to me, cocked her equine head, masseter muscles in extreme cords. With a profound effort, I responded.

—My lady, I'm familiar.

—Not as familiar as this god-serpent, watch this. Sploot yourself right there, or I'll teeth-strafe you!

In a flash, the dragon star appeared in front of the pregnant woman.

—Ah, Good Afternoon! Like what I did with those brats? Care for a little pick-me-up, male-spoiled bitch?

She muscularly lifted the woman, left hand. That was around the neck, to negate the nuisance screaming. With the right arm, she made an appalling "T" like any expert, and sinister, coroner. The sight was more than any sane human could stand, as entrails, ice-cream scooped, running with a sticky, oily squirt, spilled everywhere. A single seven-inch claw made a dark cherry wine universal. Then, Danillia bit her head off, like any guillotine, all incisors and fangs.

I couldn't believe this was happening. Then I thought to my star dragons. The 'environment' prevented me from communicating with anyone, even my weapons and Kerok-given pistols. Danillia was very thorough, and would be, all the hapless humans her result.

—Ta-da. Oh, don't worry about the others who ran, I'll just draw-and-quarter them. Thinking to my other saurian friends about my mankind-bloody-escapades? I'm sure your 'environmentally dealt with,' true? They can't escape me. You can't escape me. Nothing can. So, therefore, arrest me, Brian, I'm convicted of ultra-carnal fierceness, put the cuffs on me, for just this!

Laughing like any insane person—I mean, alien beast—the strapping reptilian gripped the pregnant woman by her arms, lifting. My jaw hit the grass, almost literally. Then the Lizardanian ripped the baby from the womb, opening the bulbous stomach with her tail. At that instance, the reptilian almost lost control of the little babe, slipping on the misplaced placenta. I stole a furtive look, seeing an infant girl, squirming into the afternoon sunlight.

—Come here you little battery-powered ballerina, wanna see what's inside a saurian? We are growing in to our opinions, yes, my sweet human?

The reptilian dropped the decapitated female and ate the infant, mercifully whole. Before she did eat it, Danillia stripped all the skin off the suckling in about two or three seconds. I was appalled to hear the *tot* <u>not</u> scream at being so graphically skinless, but howl like a benighted wolf cub. The star dragon then chewed on the ambilocal cord, just for a carnal dessert.

—My goodness, it's just like eating spaghetti, only tastier, too! Much better than the other three. Did you know my otherwise insatiable appetite is <u>increased</u> with all this violence, and all this killing of human flesh? Oh, it's just the Velociraptor in me, can't get away from my DNA, my outrageous muscles, giantess teeth, arms that could crush the Empire State Building to shreds, my talons are mega-spears, oh, its gross-out-gorgeous, right Brian?

—The other three?

—You see, simian, a couple of the 54 were pregnant. One didn't even know it. I corrected her! And when she <u>knew</u> she'd killed another human presenting herself before me, I…*corrected* them both. I felt like a Vermont schoolteacher, remember those times, my monkey-boy? Did that baby squirm like a slimy salmon! And if I can get closer to God, (if there is any) by eating human brains, Brian, well, <u>why not</u>?

Quick as any wink, the two adults hunted down, crunched to the dirt before me by magic alone. The suffering on their faces was obscured by my tears. I was crying now, couldn't help them.

Increasing her size slightly, another surprise was in order. The dragon star mounted the first flabbergasted human like copulation was going to occur.

—Oh, don't worry Brian. My companion human can give me satisfaction, be assured of that. Set your picadilloes down, you ludicrous kid. This creature is just—in my way. What spirit does my little human pet possess? Let's just see, lemme see some <u>soul</u>!

Both human legs had talons run through them. That delighted Danillia. Then, the screaming started. Not to my monster-mini-dinosaur's liking. She squashed every head like a water-filled balloon. Then she literally ripped-up the now-silent animals, with a disgusting squishing making me want to hurl.

Danillia drew her legs and fingers back and out, splitting the corpse's appendages with a loud rip. The brain, however, had been hammered in advance, just another shredded crimson-sponge.

—Tattered and threadbare for humans is a saurian-right, right Brian? I'll get the other parent with a regular draw-and-quartering, not even the mightiest Clydesdale will have anything on me, I'll show you the way to properly engage the brain and the spinal cord to register the extreme amount of worldly pain. Oh, shoot, the brains already kicked-off. Too bad. How do you feel, when I kill, Brian, makes you want to yak, right? Is this saurian acting without God, really defying Him? You humans kill 600 rabbits a day at some gang-banging-in-her-stomach-slaughterhouses? Bunny paws sold as good luck charms? God knows how many cows, pigs, chickens, and whatever you guys kill? And you lament at my killing some worthless, backwards kids-n-parents? I could have arm-squished all these shit-brats to death, breaking their stupid necks, but I had mercy, right? I smushed almost all of them with these boulders. Isn't that forgiveness enough? Those twin-asteroids, the Twins of Triton, were large enough to just finish everyone off in a mere whim! And you and that gods-damn Russian girl (at least, a piece of her) prevented it from happening. Well! I'll give you back all you lost. Does existence have any meaning at all? I'll give my answer. It's *narcissistic discompassion* of all mankind (with some exceptions). Throw up now, I command it.

At this point, I was up chucking this morning's breakfast. Mind, completely blown away. Just automatic. Danillia seemed triumphant, watching me, down on the ground, as any animal.

—You think about these children, that my torturing, agonizing a little kid can hinder me, a dragon star? Obviously, you don't understand the alien life of us. Metalaw overthrown? I thought Clare and Lara could teach you *at least* that. Sure, you have your "own" Metalaw out there, somewhere? It's only a reflection of you, you humans, coming back on an alien species, you dumb shit. You feel for nothing. When it comes to humans, I feel for nothing. The main flaw with Metalaw? It's anthropocentric, duh! It's all 'based' on your own dumb selves. So, you give a damn about these kids? I don't. I'm going to destroy millions, brats, women your miscellaneous 'innocent man' (all dozen of them). As a for-instance, when your high, through drugs, your happy. Happy, right? That emotion is what you live for, see, that dopamine? You are hedonists, all. Then, when they are gone, when the 'high' is over, then they (the drugs) are evil. Evil! You look back at this dependency on those drugs and you lament, but what are you doing? If you're so hopped-up on methamphetamine, why do we need Adderall (at all)? It's the peddler's choice, see? Why do you think all those pharmacists are <u>satisfied</u> with their stupid jobs? They sample, dumbass! This is thesis, antithesis and synthesis coming together in your very brain, Brian. You're so simple, so very simian, you don't understand. I'll show you suffering you can't believe, so watch and learn. And why am I so cruel? What can motivate a creature with my galaxy-collapsing-and-expanding mind to do such? To be so punishing, harsh, hard-core, brutal, callus, unkind, unnatural, mean and nasty? Because I <u>fucking</u> feel like it! I'll eat, sexually or otherwise, the whole lot of you humans, and just <u>forget</u> the taste of you. All humans have too much preservatives to be any good. 'Do as thou wilt,' right? I'm an anarchist, and I'll decide what <u>cruelty</u> really is. And you mere monkeys? I'll eat your brains (my little Brian) at any Manchu Han Imperial Banquet, which I'll set up. I'd kill God, I'd kill the Devil, good that they don't <u>show up</u>, because they are just sad-fucking-fiction. You creatures are ants beneath my powerful, iron heel. Your religious shit has nothing for me. All is 'known'? Don't be fooled. Mankind is a buffet set-out for the Master of Dread. Hellraiser and that Aleister Crowley fool? I'll show you ultra-Hell and Crowley's just my idiot road-<u>die</u>!

At this complete lunacy, I thought Danillia needed to be committed, and that immediately.

What asylum could hold her?

There are <u>none</u> that can.

Could her 'devotion' to anarchism be a defense? Now I was convinced that dragons couldn't be on this Earth. The crazy creature underneath me was only one of the reasons why. Would Crocodilians be any better? We didn't need naked nuclear war, some accident or dictator or sociopath somewhere? If a single Crocodilian could do this, my God, what had I done, trying to save humankind? Shit the reverse was done. All benighted me, then: I'd created a collection of future-monsters.

As the dragon star reached China, off the shores of Taiwan, right across from it, 130 or 140 miles away my full-dread cindered me (to a dragon-crisp). Didn't China think of Taiwan as a 'rogue' province? China hates things 'out of order'? You'd think Danillia wanted her arrival to be no big deal. Not so. She wanted everyone to bow, that's right <u>bow</u>, to her superior saurian entrance.

And <u>bow</u> all Chinese did, and that instinctively, automatically. Where the 'good' saurians were, I didn't know. Immediately I wished I'd had Sheeta here, or Jing Chang and some of their friends, but no! They'd gone off with their companions, leaving Earth. They didn't want to see the saurian companions corrupted by mankind's degraded ways. They knew what humans could be. If they'd known what a crazy dragon really was, I'm sure they'd be here.

Danillia arrived in China with a meaningful flourish. She was about business, something I couldn't foresee, but I did expect the worst. The Chinese had Danillia in the Great Chinese Hall and were at sixes-and-sevens about <u>what</u> to do with the magnificent but evil, beast. A dragon star visiting China, and without their companion, Jing Chang? Thing was, that wasn't the companion to Jing, but I couldn't address it, for the obvious reasons.

Unfortunately, the Chinese had a hard time communicating with Danillia. The saurian had no patience at all. She insisted that everyone supplicate before her, just like all Sovereigns. Hastily, they set up a Royal Throne Room for her, at a hellish speed. Human manpower dispensed with got a dragon huff and a bored wave from her threatening claws. Was this saurian one of the 'Cast Down,' a 'Watcher,' an 'Archangel'? At any rate, a wrathful dragon commanded, they were at sixes and sevens to comply.

—Ah! Good afternoon! What ceremony else? What are your servile wishes today? Come on, come on get going, you piggy pigs! Make your foolish entreaties!

At length, not mastering *Universalian*, but trying to, they communicated their distress over the "aircraft carriers" off the coast of China. Danillia, resting on the thronal base, only an hour-old, suddenly stood to her nine-foot height, seizing <u>two</u> officials off their feet by their lapels. She shook them rigorously. All the Chinese leaders looked on ridiculously. I just stood in one corner, totally embarrassed, thinking hard, and getting nowhere. The wistful Chinese consider me just a court jester. They couldn't be more right. Danillia's 'environment' still surrounded me, I could do nothing but observe. I'd never felt so inept as a companion before. Thing was, I was <u>not</u> the companion to Danillia. That role belonged to Jason Shireman. Strategically, maybe purposefully, he was not around.

—Speak, fools, what are you trying to say? Just before I spill your bile and insides over this nice red rug?

Shaking them vigorously like a child with an unruly doll. They indicated that Taiwan and Japan were 'enemies.' And that's all Danillia needed to hear. She accepted the 'mission' with bloody zest. Accordingly, she threw the minor officials out of the far window with a crash. Danillia had no more concern for them, just like a sociopath should. Whirling turn, she seized me.

—We've work to do; come on, sit on me and enjoy the festival and no flatulence, or I'll fist your sphincter!

She turned, of a huge sudden. In that whirl, Danillia strategically splattered me all over the floor with her mighty arm. A 60+ inch Herculean might, five foot across and around, met my head, flattening me. It felt like running into raised iron, draconian steel, completely at Danillia's (controversial) mercies. She didn't even let her 'environment' defend me.

—Goodness me! Diddum's 'fall down'? Are my fantastic biceps too beaucoup for you? Come here, you disreputable teenager.

She nonchalantly raised me up, just a sterling fork sticking nuisance-meat, pasting me on her muscular back. A grabbing saurian hand, as big as my whole chest, cleaved around me, not caring about the fang-like nails digging in.

I had no idea what to do, sadly 'pasted' on the sinews of a lunatic saurian. The entrance roof of the Great China Hall just blew off. Danillia rose and then rose again: A giant, winged dragon star, growing well-past Godzilla.

—It's time for my greatest performance yet, attend! Our aircraft carriers await. And now, last act, my final stallion-powered-fire! As for grabbing you, and my claws <u>clawing</u> you, my Rights begin where your Rights end. And I've Rights over everything, the Alpha and the Omega, hence your presence on my divine back. You know what they say about Taiwan and Japan, right Brian? I'm going to <u>trash-shit</u>! You think that Genotdelian was the Devil, well, Devil this! To hell with all this anime, right my captured human? You won't believe it, prepare to lose your lunch again. If you splatter on me, however, I'll eviscerate you. Betelgeuse, beware!

The star dragon took to the sky, and at 6,000 feet, she acted. Danillia launched, rocketed a fire as hot as any mega-sun, right at Japan, with orange, yellow and a subtle green, inundating all the islands with a flicker of flame rising, then mashing down into Taiwan. That was over 1,300 miles away, but the draconian mega-burst landed true, submerging and engulfing that whole nation in a Tsar Bomba field of unimaginable inferno.

—No big deal, the Japanese Islands are up in a fireball reaching the outer atmosphere and then, why, we'll get started! Look at Taiwan, 'the darkness of the death bird was blown away,' right Bri? Wouldn't that just make Sheeta Miyazaki and Nausicaa Lee's day? Shame we can't bring them into our story for tearful lament! Look at all these Asians, horrifically dead as winter mud. Just think, all this with one Lizardanian spell, to keep those loser dragons in their self-satisfied darkness, while the whole Earth suffers my wrath. If the saurians knew of my power over them all, with the exception of Soreidian, this is the Power of Ruse, I'd be Outcast from the Earth. But then, where would all the <u>fun</u> be?

Danillia strained herself, poising for the Eastern World to see, doing a Hulk-stier, I knew that this was one of the most muscle-overloaded-females that ever was. The saurian stationed herself on the top-most building in Beijing, looking at the raging fire consuming Japan, and, with her eagle eyes, the same-self decimating Taiwan. This was my thousandth time I regretted climbing on her enstrengthened back. Danillia's massive arms were the size of a football field. Her whole body, Olympian muscle times 100(0).

—Add an additional '0' on the end of the last sentence, too. I also got all the 120,000 visitors to Japan, an added bonus on our humanitarian tragedy (if your me). I can't believe I didn't start this in Book One, what was I doing? I really <u>did</u> mean to do it. Littorian, Korillia, Clareina, Larascena, and the other dumb ass lizards and worms aren't here to defend you. Oh, of the people I just wiped out of existence, didn't you feel their souls 'passing' (by)? Sort of like passing gas, and if I feel some caressing my muscled, Pegasus-strong-back, I'll paddle your ass with nine-inch nails. I'll rip you to tatters in any evening breeze. Sometimes a cigar is just a cigar—say that to 'yon phallus,' right? Some think your loins 'deliver' your soul into others? For me, well, that could be right. Too bad that humanity is on my dinner plate, and I've just had a great serving. Well, that takes care of Taiwan and Japan. Two ships sunk by my ultra-saurian-firepower. I'm satisfied with my 125 million Japanese killed and 24 million Taiwanese obliterated. Forward to snuffing you, Brian Miller Human, it's about past-time, don't you think? As you see, the human public was not shocked, literally no one did anything. No one has even noticed the extinguishment of all these humans? The Japanese islands, all of them, completely destroyed and a saurian spell covering it all up. Isn't it fantastic? Isn't a Lizardanian's magic majestic? I mean, we don't know magic instinctively, as thoroughly as an Alligatorian does, but some of us are trying. The 'newness' of it all: All humanity was possessed by this spell. Can I contain it all within my web-of-magic? Look at all that luggage and cell phone shitbaggyness? Should be thrilling to see how long my spell will last...but NOT for you, attend!

The dragon rose, returning the way we'd come, the Pacific Ocean passing by. Then something occurred to me. I was Danillia's prisoner, no doubt there. Thing is, she was a female. Maybe, just maybe, the same kind of intimacy I had with Larascena and Clareina could be utilized on Danillia. I leaned over to her, again countenancing her saurian eye.

—My Esteemed lady, you know me well?

—Well enough just before I destroy you utterly.

—Very good, my Empress. You know about my shortening everything down, due to my simian nature?

—I know about that. We must be tolerant of our pets. Since you'll be destroyed soon, it doesn't matter. At least, not to me.

—Great then, my Eminence. Then let's further impose. May I call you "Danny," for short, my notorious and Mega-Brutal Queen?

She blinked, my 'shortening' being solicited just on her. The complement she shrugged off. Thinking of obliterating the ameba on her back, Danillia giggled.

—Danny? You want to call me *Danny* now? Hu(man) you really need to be killed, thank the gods, it will be by me. Didn't you know my name was already shortened in *Universalian* to appease your teenage predilections? Just for that, I'd like to squeeze my hands into your little mouth and open your jaws to dislocation and maybe beyond that? Easy, peasee! Oh, such, such were the joys! That way you'd bleed out so slowly? As an added bonus, I'll just consume your blood, to get the energy out of you, Clare, Lara and Littorian, my little willing reverse-vampires, right? What do you call Littorian, for short? 'Litt,' perhaps? As in 'Little'? I've an added-additional beef with you, he should not be Lord of the Lizardanians. Oh, alright, for now. You've my permission, I'll be your "Danny," and your demise.

Another spell possessed Danillia then, the Monologue Ghost seized the ultra-Velociraptor. Once again, as Japan and Taiwan burned to a mere cinder below us, Danny turned herself around. I felt the tell-tale scales sliding by, and the massive hands moving up to my hips.

—And we will finish with yon hipsters if you—

—But my lady! What of the Dyatlov Pass Incident?

—The what? What's that? Speak up!

—I've not told you of that, my Ruler? How rude of me not to mention that, please let me explain. Could you squish me hereafter, oh, that's better my lady. Can you turn back around? Oh, that's going too far, well in 1959, a group of nine, fit, dexterous young people went into the Ural Mountains of Russia and horror was to follow. I give to you, my mighty (and please, merciful) saurian Ideal, the Dyatlov Pass incident. And how can I tell you of this story? Well, it's through the camera pictures and on-site journals. We actually know what happened to these youthful skiers, as you'll hear. At the Ural Polytechnical Institute ten students really wanted "grade three," the most prestigious hiking certificate in all the Soviet Union, and this is their motivation to go. They left any kind of drugs and stuff like that behind, you know, like Vodka and cigarettes, so serious was this sojourn. Their goal: Reach the mountain of Goro Orton, listed at the top of difficulty. On the 25th of January, they started out. So, where are we, my Gracious Queen?

—Ah, we are almost at the Marshall Islands, but speak on, Hawaii, my destination-next from there, I'll have me a ton of Hawaiian Bowls, too, about a million and a half people, I can see those humans sizzling, too bad you won't be around to see it.

—My Atlantis-mighty-and-superior-saurian, it follows hard upon. Hawaiian Bowls, wow, good plan! Dyatlov mentioned to Yuri that he'd send a message back, a telegram—

Danillia grew anxious.

—What's a telegram, be quick!

Danillia hadn't got her massive hands off my hips, and she shook me, seeking an answer.

—My dearest lady, it's like, uh, a message? Stop shaking this noddle out, please, so I can continue?

Only slightly satisfied, Danillia was urgent.

—Proceed, then, proceed!

The dragon star was growing antsy, not a good sign for me. She had a habit of cracking her massive knuckles, sounding like a thunderstorm, and she did so again. Then, she moved them back to my middle section, tightening slightly.

—Yes, my Eminence. Well, that tele—that message—never came, because something really went wrong, as you'll detect. Anyhow, Yuri Yudin's backing-out saved his very life. There were then seven men and two women. Igor Dyatlov was in charge of the group. He was respected and well-informed, a good leader. Because it was January and February, the weather was bad, see, my lady? Yudin reported the group as missing so by the end of February, a search party when to Dead Mountain, or Silent Peak, or, as known by the Mansi people, who lived there, as Kholat Syakhl. The rescuers located the tent alright. But the tent was cut open from the inside!

At this, I got down level with her huge, wild, and (really) yearning eyes. Probably anticipating killing me, the delight it'd cause. I stared down into the dragon's massive left orb. You wouldn't think a saurian face can be muscular, but it definitely was. Green, blue, and a little yellow, fought in a defined-eyelid-stream trying desperately to show their dominance over everything and everyone. Years, no eons, of amazing strength rippled and pulsed between and beneath those scales around her amazing, Equestrian head. Many more years than either Lara or Clare, I thought, with a siring lump in my throat. Years were revered in saurians, the older the (far) better. Still, she fitfully waited, all enraptured with my story. "Danny" said whimsically this:

—When you give your 'opinion,' when you 'opine' on something, you have to respect those who would listen to you, star dragons will listen because you're a companion, your Littorian's companion, see? It's position, not really story. All connections? You bet it's true, even among us reptilians. You're not being a genius, you're being a secret dope, and the longer you keep dragon stars here, the more your people are biting the brink of a shit sandwich. 'Course now, it's too late.

—So please you, Danny, can I go on?

—Yes, yes. Pre-unbeknownst to you, I'll get you back for that Name-Shortening-Shinola, but speak on, why don't you?

—They were scared so badly, they slashed their own tent. All nine of the hikers were found, in the appalling snow, leading away from the tent sight. None were dressed for the negative 30 below-zero temperature. Organized, and single file walking, and that was strange indeed. The bodies were found in the trees, and the trekkers were mangled. Hypothermia was the cause of death, but that isn't the whole story.

Bodies were moved, and then the searchers found Igor Dyatlov. He was found face up, both hands made into fists, as though he was fighting somebody—or some...thing! He was cut up, cut up bad, and missing his jaw incisor. All of the hikers were very messed up, fighting something much stronger than any human. Radiation was a factor in this too. This was all caused by...

At this, I stayed silent.

—By what? Come human don't leave me hanging or I'll definitely hang you!

—The military. The military killed them all, because these hikers were very near...

—Near what, what, come on you gorilla-gerbil-bottom-feeder?

—A wormhole, my lady. The Soviet Military had uncovered a wormhole and they still don't know what it really is. It's in a cave, on Dead Mountain. They secretly want a dragon star, maybe even <u>you</u>, to come out there and explain it all to them. This wormhole might lead into the past. So, where are we now?

—Don't worry about it. Let me hear the conclusion to the Dyatlov Pass Incident, my sub-simian. I've a secret spell to bring you back from the Dead (if applied quick enough). And you definitely don't want this spell—it will make you welcome your end. You know what L.R. Brower said: 'Perfection comes from just existing.' Let's just see if that's true. Death Incarnate might find you, and you can still die by violence. For now, I'll decide when and where you die.

Danillia squeezed my hips together with her unmatchable hands-and-claws (with some delight), then, of a sudden, she noticed me smiling.

—I know it's a bad omen, just when I'm about to overcome all the saurian cherry in you, watching it burst asunder, when skin is cut wide open, but why are you grinning, gorilla-face?

—A moment to answer, your highness?

—Ah, that's granted.

Looking briefly around, they were over the Marshall Islands, 3,000 feet up, her wings majestic, gliding on the smooth sky, Danillia <u>did</u> relax her grip just barely.

—I would tell you the tale of <u>The Terror</u> (and the Her Majesty's Ship Erebus), which would mesmerize you again, only you don't have time to hear it.

—I'll be the judge of time here, ass-scratcher.

—At least I've got <u>my</u> evolutionary ladder intact, which is strange. And Strangely Enough, that you do not?

A spirited reply did not issue from the reptilian just then. I was whisked away, seemingly by magic. It was Kerok, the wisest Alligatorian and he literally saved my life, him swooping down from on-high. Katrina was my orchestrator. I wonder if she's getting tired of doing that? She got the magic-induced dragons to <u>see</u> what was going on. It took some time. But she did it. Danillia was leapt-on by furious dragon wings, knocking her bodily down into the Marshall Islands by three sets of wanton talons. Larascena, Clareina and Littorian had arrived. The thunder crack alone could have deafened anyone. The supremely surprised Danillia was "descended" to Eneko Island, as Lucifer brought down to Earth.

Only intervention from Soreidian and the cream of the saurians' 20 Lizardanians saved Danillia, then. They had a spaceship standing by and all of them were gone. Larascena, Clareina and Littorian just let them go, and good riddance. I just nonchalantly blew it all off as Danillia being in a mood, brightly smiling to the downcast (but friendly) dragon stars.

They had a lot of work to do.

It took them well over a month, but the saurians <u>did</u> do it. All of this reptilian destruction, they brought back. Japan was a miracle, but they timed it so the annihilation, for those returned from the nether world, never really happened. Same with Taiwan and all the destruction Danillia caused. All the 'tourons' when back into a normal, bourgeoisie existence. Teresian was suggesting they go back in time, but hesitance was the rule. The punishment was that Danillia couldn't return to Earth—and any saurian could see (or not see) to that end! Not a bad punishment in Danillia's estimation. She hated, really hated me. She should have finished me, but my damn, canonizing, stories! They delayed her.

Oh, the defeat of dragons due to their silly, diminutive whims; puzzles and stories, physical pride in themselves, a 'little thing' in gems, action without thinking ahead, and (the notorious) wishing themselves as God (sometimes forgetting, conveniently, the small 'g').

In fact, no Alligatorians nor Lizardanians would be on Earth much longer. I thought my salvation would be in friendship with the Crocodilians and, maybe, the Wysterians. While there were only TWO Wysterians, if you really knew them, well, it'd be more than enough. I had Asians in charge of that, I trusted them, again cutting against the grain. But of my Danny, I shuttered, if she was alive in the Universe...

...she'd get me.

And by violence, too, even in our sleep, it's a 'violent act' if you really think about it. Danny would get me.

And any *fool* can see that.

~~PART TWO~~

We, Carcosa

I return

A sub-hero of a pirate victory

A plunderer of God's precious time

Betrayed by the enemy's scorn for my awesome power

I find

That I'm just a little warrior

Dipping a thimble in a sea of blood and fear

Where waves grow old and life is small

And Death is no longer exquisite

History has abandoned me on this savage cliff

Where those blinded gulls fly overhead

Their wings blood-soaked with the conflicts of a thousand banners

I realize now that what HAPPENED

was not for me

I should have staved off the compulsion to war

through such expendable days

I would have better stayed home

to tend the cabbages and clip the roses

and drink the nectar of another spring

Instead, I took <u>ORDERS</u>

and hoisted the banner of my empire

I did as I was <u>TOLD</u>

each hour, day and night...

—FROM THE POEM, <u>WAR NO MORE</u> AUTHOR UNKNOWN

A series of Black Holes and White Holes, dealing with Time the way dragons *just did*—and the planet appeared below us. Arriving at the sphere Lizardania, of a <u>massive</u> sudden, the kidnapping star dragon opened her prodigious mouth. I could see the fiendish fangs, aimed toward the nuisance, and retreating, star ship. We three humans on the creature's sinewy back crouching down between her five-foot fins. Already and always, nothing we could do. A terrific flame came from her lungs, between her elongated incisors, a twine of yellow, orange and green super-flame, like someone <u>spitting</u> between their teeth. Jezebellian zeroed-in on the retreating craft, for another raw lick of extreme fire. It broke and snapped through the cigar-like structure like a sheering and splintering rope. Her fire obliterated any and all shieldings or deflectors, sending the hapless spaceship down to a small island. Individuals—alien, otherwise—hurried out. All had laser guns. Brian busted out.

—My lady, have mercy, maybe they are—

—Shut up, you 'tarded toad, *this morning is mine*! I'm Jezebellian, the Lizardanian, this mission, <u>*is I*</u>! Don't care <u>who</u> they are. What punishment isn't a blessing presented by a saurian? Let's get some burned toast started!

Laser guns hit the 'environment' cast over us by Jezebellian, to no avail, of course. Nothing (known) could get through this saurian radiance, the 'environment' she had covering her riders. Simulating a Stuka bomber, the reptilian dove down, belting a mastodon blaze, unimaginable. All on the island, consumed in dragon fire, enflamed everybody to a suitable (near) crisp. It was intensely hot, but not molten, allowing a *painful* time to burn. Absolutely no survivors. All the humans aboard her can attest, the dragon star was a *sinuous block*, a brick house, mighty-mighty as the song goes. This reptilian rivaled Danillia in terms of physique. And this saurians' guns? Any gargantuan slabs of enormous visceral force, aching for any kind of action-pack. Brian spoke, after seeing the outrageous calamity.

—My lady, what if they were friendly?

—You've got to be Lincoln Logging me! I'd duly slaughter, friendly or no, and rightly that. Besides-and besides, no one is 'friendly' to me. I've a mission and you're on it, dipstick! I kill where and how I like; nothing can oppose this dragon (star!). God, I'm a millionaire dragging an anchor, goddamn human beasts. Like I said family: To Carcosa, my pre-tortured humans. And Danillia proved herself, evoking another spell on our pleasant sucker worms, eh, Brian? You know the old (recent) human saying: "Fool me once, shame on you; you can fool me, 'can't get fooled again!" Those *squillionaires* were so focused on Danillia, I just 'slipped' in. Pun intended. Cast a spell on all those dorks. And Danillia conjuring up 'a Double' of Brian Miller, too! Two saurians, two spells. We are not GOOD at it, but, with study…yes, we are! He's wrecking everything back yonder. Danillia and I only know a few bewitchments, her sorcery, limited. She observed you, Brian Miller, on a deeper level, hence a suitable necromancy. Here, as a Lizardanian, I can't produce anything like a Crocodilian can, when it comes to fire. Wasn't it fun to watch them burn slowly, the fools below on that shitty island? Let's stay on course, though, I've taken <u>orders</u>. Danillia, she's one I really owe. In a sparring match, she could have killed me. She didn't. Getting the humanesque growths on my back to their torment session, then I'm free of that worm-bitch. The favor I owed her, now *penetrated* fully, or will be, right my kidnapped Brian and friends?

Jezebellian malevolently *talked street*, far more than Danillia did. I didn't know what Brian's doppelganger was doing back on Earth. My thoughts were being gathered up, by the wily serpent.

—Yes, that's right Michael. My 'Double' is getting divorced from the saurians, <u>shitting</u> on his companion, making a mockery of all human confidantes everywhere, causing a nuclear war (or two), scatting right in the Crocodilian's mouths and all the rotten deeds that even YOU can't imagine, I've no time to think about all of them. Danillia had a 'Double' of Brian Miller go and raise mayhem on Earth, while I, Jezebellian 'dispose' of the real Brian! Ain't it cool? Mark that down, a great enchantment by your local dragons.

That froze Brian and me. Marco didn't really care, because he didn't believe any of it. Maybe (hopefully) he was right!

—Carcosa is on the other side of Lizardania. We will get there very soon. First, let's play (the end) of the game?

Jezebellian had to set things right with Brian Miller. Every one of us, me, (the author), Marco and Brian, lost in a whopping can of WD-40. We slid on the serpents prodigious back just as if she were...a snake! Her abdominals under us, a rollercoaster of extreme muscles. Both Marco and I sighed at such appalling mightiness. The creature was more than a Velociraptor with iron wings, she was a sculpted mountain of raw unexpurgated power.

—No death shroud for you, Brian. Lemme see those yon hipsters, pray? Time to *bulwark* this out.

The Lizardanian broke Brians hips in nine places, POP, POP, POP, POP—damn, you *more* than get it. Squishing a brown banana, we watched in awe. The agony Brian felt was unthinkable. Marco and me, well, we weren't exactly heroes, looking at the waves.

—Now then, my injured Brian. As expected, your saurian resistance was no match for my power. I don't give a damn how much dragon blood you've drunk (or drank?). It wouldn't have been a challenge to Danillia, either. If she'd gotten down to business. Yes, it did require some strength, you're only a pre-dragon, you cum-dumpster Brian. The *pain* you just felt is nothing. The AI you fear will be the AI that kills you in the end. Let's hurry to my "Dragon-Andies." They'll be so happy to see you again. Soreidian approved all of this, by-the-bye-the-buy? Understand he's revisited Carcosa repairing those Andies, yes? Revenge their watchword. My sole question, just this: Was it worth all the *trouble*, Bri?

Brian immediately took his hands off his midsection. That almost brought out in additional cry. He held it in. Brave (and reckless) to the last. In an anxiety of hurt, the companion smiled into Jezebellian's muscularly carved countenance, down on her left, a grin into that crafty (and crazy) blue, green, yellow and fitful orb.

—My goodly and peppy lady, given my wives? The *joy* of those hours? What trouble? Uh, my uniquely, kidnap—

Then I pushed Brian Miller from my position in the middle. Marco nodded, with a well-meaning pat on my shoulder.

—Ah, the saurian Love Machine. Guess I can't match the warm iron vice of two priss vices? Oh, well. It's an end of anarchy even I can't understand, *brought to you by* human scum skeeting on the basement bathtub.

—My Esteemed lady, I've no base—

—Expression, dumb shit. Hey, Marco: You believe in Saurian Anarchy?

Marco thought, actually releasing one of her lengthy fins, as the saurian turned back around. Marco scratched his chin.

—My lady…I'd better!

—Brief. Good. You get a pass, for the moment. Michael and Brian should learn something. Your 'portability' is forgiven, too. J. Michael Brower isn't far behind you, maybe he's the same weight. Brian Miller (have your hips recovered by now?), is in, very regrettably, dragonesque shape, enough 'bout him. By the way, I've something *against* the author, 'exposing' the saurians. I've something special for you. We'll get to it.

I spoke, seemingly for everyone.

—That's profoundly perceptive of you, my reptilian lady. That's what the scab kids at school always say. I do talk (and write) awkwardly.

Conceded. Uh, can we have a break, just at this little island, no, not the scorched one, just there, speaking of emptiness? Guy has needs, my Sovereign.

As a wink, the dragon landed. The humans did what they had to do. Jezebellian waited, looking at the sand, rather blankly, and not, NOT thinking. Not thinking about what she was doing. Not thinking about who it affected. Not really...thinking. She had a mission to do. In seven minutes, airborne again.

—Thank you my lady.

—Satisfied, my hairless?

—No. 2 for me and Marco. Don't know about Brian.

—Uh-huh. How drunk are you, Michael? Had your 'toddy' today or are you thinking about your recent 'potty,' 'venture? You ole skeeted _booze_hound. And that rhymes with your home country today: An adventure in _shitfaced shoplifting_. Mighty lucky you've 'wears' to catch your filth on, or I'd have splatted you over the field and beyond, Danillia assignment be damned. Keep your sphincter puckered up, ya hear, mashed John Barleycorn?

—At least we've our priorities straight, my lady. I do think Michael's just a Student Alcoholic, not an advanced case, my Queen-Monarch?

That came from Marco.

—Keep it up, maggot. Back to our waterlogged Feculence King. Michael: Smacked you soaked boozer?

—Pretty inebriated, my lady, can't really stand up (I acknowledge to God I'm sitting down!). Thanks for that reference to Jack London, there. Could use a refill, kinda dry?

Of a sudden (_real_ sudden!) Jezebellian just went OFF on the author, or maybe, all of us occupying the 'chain of command' over ALL life on Earth?

—This first: J. Michael Brower, what a miserable life. Ended (or started?) in the Pentagon when you were 18 years old? All through a ruse?

The Luevano Outstanding Scholar Program? You're in your own category, that's for the gods-sure. Boy, if they could SEE you now...old, fat, grey and in the way. Parents divorced at 11? Typing saved you. And you are STILL typing, not really composing a god-s-damn *meaningful phrase*! Isn't that what Ernest Hemingway tried to do, compose one meaningful sentence? No wonder he killed himself, as all 'meaningful' writers (just) do: Virginia Woolf, Hunter Thompson, Robert E. Howard, shall I go on? Air Force at 19—went to West Germany and a GLCM Warrior, too? Ground Launched Cruise Missiles? And wasted your subsequent life as an Immigration Officer? Then you stupidly went back to the Pentagon for eight or nine years? Then Justice Department, what a laugh. That became Homeland Security after 9/11. Detention and Deportation? You stole this land now taking it from other people? All mankind came over the Bering Strait, now covered with ocean, so no one is a "Native" born, all from Deepest, Darkest? Yike and yuck, so typical, I don't care to explore it further. What'd be the point? Yeah, you wrote, and a lot, too, ho-screwball-hum. Like Dan Cragg said, you're not a writer unless paid. Royalties and checks, you're a writer! Stroke at 38 and *now* what are you? Can't find the words? Oh, poo! Go with Charles Bukowski and 'do something else'! I had to raid your custodial facility at that crappy Portland State University for *little you*? Doing the 'top floors' of a building going to the hounding dogs? And got your boss, your supervisor, too, right, Marco? In a conversation about 'being a custodian'? I shit on philosophy all over the place. Damn your city is a Netherworld of drugs, everyone wasted on something tomorrow! Gods, I'm so sick of the things you don't know. And this guy, this writer, a prisoner of *Liquid Courage*? Drunk? Couldn't defeat your wife in a hand-to-hand struggle, right? What a priss! That 'street' enough for you, you rotten criticizers, you faultfinders??? Oh, how I wish I could be there to see it! Maybe she'd lift you up in her gargantuan hands, right? Throw you out the window? Least you'd get some 'touching' then, right? She's a journeywoman carpenter? Like to see you smashed all over the street, mercy of the gawking neighbors? You see all this as a World War One journey, barrels of wine nulling your brain for an "Over the Top" garbage dumping and cleaning out your pissers and shitters? Lucky you were a captain...once? I don't know which is worse. Your wife is, well, what _all_ wives are only a whole lot more so. Neither of you guys, Michael and Marco seemed surprised to see me? That was a little queer. I've learned a few quotes in life, coming to the 'university' of the vermin: "Slavery was never abolished it was only extended to include all the colors." Charles Bukowski, ah, yes, an 'emotional' human. He would have done better than you two thinking about what's really happening. And what is happening? Anyhow, you both better hope for death. You'll get it, sadly, _not_ quickly. Your fingers go to sleep as your typing, right, Micky? Bad circulation, no doubt. Had to put that in, Brian's shortening names down to...nothing? Almost 60 years-(so)-old-my-has-been-writer? And you with your 'teenagers and star dragons'. What'd your wife say, haven't they just 'dissipated' yet? She can't read a word of your writing, like, anytime? All too disjointed and fucked up for her, eh? An anvil sliding into a greasy noose, that's the result. News for you, your wife holding the rope open for your obese neck. We, the saurians, give solace to your clowning, ram- (and Rum) shackled, flippant life. Like your wife says, she "can't hardly" read the miserable stuff you came out with. And 'publish' at _your_ expense? I mean, you could talk about the publisher in this piece, and no one would be the wiser. What a pathetic joke. Your stupid words will be an unheard saurian whisper of any wind when we finally go. Damn you, Michael, for writing of the Elder gods anyway. And the shit we've told you? Thankfully no one will read it. You're so blown away; you don't even remember it. Everything left is gravy, at your pre-grave-end? And your rabbits? And the 'known' Sunflower House? It's YOU who are the WORM, NOT any saurians you might meet, Mr. hand jobber. Look at your weak and weakening body. Your wife thinks, why _are_ you, why are you _EVEN_ alive? She will celebrate the day _you_ die. Like Job's wife said, curse God and die?

Wormwood for me. You drink so much that when you hit the bathroom, you dripple a little water on your pants from piss bleeding through. And no one *could tell* when you walk out, thinking you just wiped your hands on your trousers? Leave a room NICER than when you entered it. Ah, saurian wisdom never known by your shitty (literally) people. You could never exit a room brighter than rainbows, right? Boy, I'd like to see you in diapers as an old(er) man. Know this, as well. I *saw* what you wrote. At the beginning? Your little ode to poetry, up top, previous pages? Because, maybe, your Mother was President of the Michigan Poetry Society? Like anyone cares! "PRAISE THE NOTCHES ON MY CARBINE STOCK!" Who EVEN gives a shit? A saurian CAN'T care. You tried that 'poesy' stuff in other books, just an amateur affair. This is a society of SHOPLIFTERS, not a profound higher-level civilization. Everyone 'capitalizes' off everyone else, sickest thing in a debauched society. Yes, you joined the military. At the 'tender age' of 19? Veteran now? That's BECAUSE there was NO WAY OUT! That's WHY you 'joined.' The same age as the 'average recruit' in Vietnam I understand? Vietnam has NEVER been defeated. Know why? Because EVERYONE participates, and that, always. Women, kids, adults. And now they make T-shirts, and Nike-things-of-nabobs and whatever else for the Capitalist Empire today? It's like you NEVER fought there at all! The asinineness of human over-all-existence! And Americans, replacing the Japanese, replacing the French, fought in Nam, for 30+ years? The 1% is to blame, eh? Ah, the "Browning of America" you can't even come out with that today, kinda 'racist' right? That's the whole thing, the Nordic Countries, with their 'whiteness,' the hierarchies—like a saurian cares at all. Jamie Johnson, in profound naivete, makes a *mockery* of the middle, lower and under class, on YouTube, right? _Born Rich_ and _The 1%_? Sorta like _War—What For?_ by George R. Kirkpatrick (1909) and _Why I Am A Socialist_ by Charles Edward Russell (1910) and _Bolshevism_ by John Spargo (1919), and _ What's So and What Isn't_ by John Work (1910) and a list of other useless books moldering away to the gnawing critique of yonder rats and mice? You just KEEP doing the same things, again and again. This or that 'Monkey' claims your <u>share</u> given to him? Or Him? Capitalizing His name, like he's your next Jesus? Rubbish! I'm up on all your impractical classics. You WANT to write something like _The Rebel_ by Albert Camus? Let me tell you, you'll never make it. Michael is consumed <right word!> by a few academics now, less every day, no one wants to read your (profound) shit. Your planet is finished, it's now awaiting the NEW-DARK-AGES! Full of radiation, resentment and vanity, <u>vanity</u>. Danillia summarized all those books for me, agonizingly went through them, <u>telepathizing</u> it to me. Gods, I did suffer that! It's like women only getting the vote in America in 1920, you think THEY need to be in 'charge'? Just when Joan of Arc became a Saint? Women WILL finish you! Thinking things will be BETTER thereafter? Don't be fooled (again). Shit for MEN it's 'all a show'; but women, *without kids*, <u>will</u> take it all VERY seriously. Seriously indeed. I don't even need to BE there when you WALK into a limited nuclear (and naked) war (which won't be 'limited'). You know who will be responsible, too. Women are superior to men; any fool can see that. They set the foundations of your ultimate destruction. Hell, you were ALL women once! Look it up on your god(s)damn Internet(s)! *Everything known?* Codswallop, claptrap and jackstraw. The women will conquer you right down into the dirt, my males. Even Socrates said it, "Once made equal to man, women becomes his superior." So, god(s)damn it, don't *make* them equal? When women do get in charge, inevitable, they say you've suffered no injury when you were in the military? In 20,000 years, men will be extinct. That's in contention now. Anyway, the gods say you'll <u>never</u> be there because of your shitty nukes! And we saurians NEED these 30, your only card. You see my boy-toys? You are damned if you do, damned if you don't *via* <u>women</u>! That's why the Germans went to war THREE times in 'recent' years on your shitty planet—because of the women. It's male <u>pride</u> that guides war via the women they must spawn with! Oh, so soon, we'll be in Carcosa. Then. I can be rid of the growths on my sinuous back, thanks to the gods. It's rotten, putrid butterfat, *that* with your water, bone and empty (and wanting) brains! As for a poison-bourbon refill, Michael, oh, believe me, I'll have a dozen AI dragons shitting down your nasty throat, soon as we get to Carcosa. Hear me, my unfortunate humans and tremble!

—My profound lady, in _War No More_ the WORD is 'IN' not 'ON,' you know, when you say, 'praise the notches 'on' my carbine stock'? It's "IN" and that's a correction to you, my Revered Queen. A carbine is a little shorter than a long gun. On the other (other?) hand, people, on a rare occasion, confuse 'notch' with—

—How <u>absolute</u> the knave is! Ah, just sit by your shitty dumb dish, writer-fool. Like Socrates said, 'I know that I know nothing!'. If he lived <u>*forever*</u>, then he'd know! YOU, SUPERVISOR? Still there?

—Yes, my…my mistress. I heard what you said. It is. Distressing. And just by the way, I'm no stranger, I'm Marco! Like I was implying, in regard to 'democracy,' such is the case with all kings, all dictators, all autocrats—

—Don't you wish 'God' as "King" ruling everybody, Marco?

—…and to the *contradiction*, my Sovereign. Better human minds have delt with this question, over the years.

—"*Delt* with this," that's right. That's a good one. Peas and carrots in a pod, do you remember grabbing our little *belletristic piffle* by his tic-tac gonads? With your legs 'blessing' my strong back? If it smells like shit, check your own boot, eh, Marco? And you my supervisor, Messrs. Marco Piscitelli, with my 'environment,' which you've no comprehension of understanding if we had 100 years of knowledge-infusion, just holding your guts in? Your just along for the ride. We'll be at Carcosa soon. Say the right thing, or SPLAT like a Hefty garbage bag down below?

Marco didn't feel like sustaining this saurians scatological talk. He endured it, to the relief of the other two humans. Marco knew that folks get hurt, when *misbehavin'* towards a dragon star. Knowing that, will get you far. It wasn't cowardice *per se*. In the shadow of this Lizardanian, this saurian, this Jezebellian, it couldn't be. Sure, she could crush him into a thousand sinister things. But even Marco couldn't compromise on some stuff. Faith, honor, independence, good tidings, happy human laughter, or his own believes. Things are evil and rotten. He *wished* to see his family again. His wife. Home. Humans, maybe Marco himself, have done things that are wrong, people get hurt just plain living, *living* with feeling, the mixed-up emotions. And everybody's got *mixed feelings*. Rich or poor, no matter. Marco's 'humanity' didn't seem like it had a place in this serpent's twisted view.

—It will be as you say, my lady.

That sparked a thought for this reptilian, just then. Dreamily, the saurian thought of 'the mission.' In ancient-times, beyond the Old Ones and when the Universe-All-Was-Young, Jezebellian sparred with Danillia. The reason didn't count. All without weapons, the two saurians fought. It wasn't a 'short fight,' it went on for years, continuously. At the end, when Jezebellian was raised up in Danillia's triumphant hands, above her fins, all energy drained from the defeated, there was mercy.

Oh, you're not too good to die, but your good enough for me: Live, my little minion, take some cure, you do need it. Do me a favor, too, no questions?

A sudden inquiry got Jezebellian out of this thousand-time sinister dream.

—My lady, how do you know this is Carcosa?

She rounded a massive eye on Brian.

—And what do you think of me, my sweet, I'm not your *modus vivendi*?

Brian, not compared to a monkey, or some such, spirited right up.

—Of you, my saurian, I think the world, my most moist, and Esteemed, gracious lady. The saurian beneath me should be set-up on high so I could worship her in an adequate fashion, your monumental, molded legs crushing my cranium at your utter whim, fondling generous hair in the meantime. My mouth, overdrive and then some. You are a god-like creature of an unrivaled knowledge and mega-ultra-strength, the model of all life, and the extremity of supremacy to all-EVERYONE, and others not in that class, and that everywhere, my mistress, (please) mine?

At this (sudden) jolt, the creature got an idea. This notion: I must have Brian Miller as *my* possession, a personal pet. This creature could be Jezebellian's own, and no other could contest it. Not even Littorian, as Jezebellian ripped this *nicety* out of the saurian's benign claws.

—Wow. Can see why...you have the wives you do; you have a velvet tongue.

—Ask you a question, my lady?

—Granted.

—You know me, may I call you 'Jezzie'?

—And you did call Danillia, 'Danny' right?

—I...did...that, lady.

Jezebellian thought.

At length, we flew over the island of sad Carcosa. The shoals and sandbars of life faded away. Formation of clouds overhead was ineffable. Thunder was gobbled up in a wind that *didn't* let it ignite. Lightning did nimble out, but brief as a human to cry, then stopping indifferently. All the lightning did do was illuminate the saurians beautiful, but strangely dreadful, face. Through the whisps over the towers, we humans could see that most of the city was underwater! It was, indeed, a metropolis, and it had a break-wall surrounding it, but that was demolished by the ceaseless, pounding, incessant waves, so only a whisp was left. There was nothing left and no visible life. Dark, but more than just dark. Cascading, like an ill-designed oil painting, pigments running down in a distorted 'rendering' of a red-shaped sub-reality. Subject matter, dark Carcosa, no one wanting to paint it again. Genius pounded and pulverized by the underfed waves. 'City of Forlornness' wouldn't have done; it was atrociously ghastly. Desolation was more to the like. What star bird has the heart to sing in sad-and-thorn-laden Carcosa? Oh, the oceans were having their annihilating affects. We humans saw Carcosa completely, something we could never Unsee. A happy lamentation of the dragon-flame-princess circling all the desolation.

Carcosa, like I said, if that really was the city's name, would be under the sea, before long. The semi-underwater town was a slow rift of absurd ruin. Years, no eons, gone sorrowfully by-and-bye. It had five fine towers, surrounding the city and three bridges, alas, almost submerged. However, all the 'fineness,' disintegrating, slowly. Like any old man on a given beach, sand-through-the-hands, until…no more. The star dragon flew around the five-mile city, and the silence reached up, giving me the shivers. The sky above the lost city was of particular interest. We flew below the rising storm. And storms were continuously rising. Several mean-spirited clouds, pregnant with rain, threatened even more water on yesterday's loneliness. All the buildings and the cottages were ripped away, in every fashion. Only the bare structures remained. A castle stood above the town, in the central part, integrating with the Draconian, bird-shunned shadows (ode to the greatness of Howard Phillips Lovecraft). Seeing the castle was like sighting a phantom, a mist all around. Water, everywhere and everywhen. Not enough to cover up the lost, dark ultra-city, but, like Global Warming, the dark water *was* getting there. The patriarch of trees grew shorter as you approached the castle. The whimsical yesterday-suns, and there were two, a lime tract around the black edges, dancing above the structure like a haunter in the darkening sky.

—You've been here before, right Brian? Sure, call me Jezzie; the robot addies will reward you Brian, soon enough. If I listen, I can almost hear you screaming.

Marco took up the rear, me in the middle (typical writer-thing) and Brian-sat-Point. Jezebellian was our conductor. If I, the author, had only seen the things she'd do, I'd wish her destruction. That's not really my style. I've adopted Littorian's phrase: *To understand all, is to forgive all.*

Brian Miller wanted to delay the Death Beetle of Carcosa.

—Cat got your veiny-bowling-balls, Bri? What have you to say to your Jezzie?

—A story to tell you, mistress. I won't take long?

To stall. That was the key. To stall the dragon? It'd worked before. Brian decided to take that risk.

—I could tell the story of the 47, but continue flying, my royal lady, Carcosa is just (a little) there.

A draconian voice, raised, in contradiction.

—What's that? Speak backyard-gorilla!

—My grace, that's the 47 Ronin of—

—What's 'Ronin' monkey?

—My Inestimable Queen, that's folks that don't have a ruler.

—A what? Human, what's that got to do with—

—Slow down, I'll tell you the story, Jezzie.

Marco and Michael, of a sudden, felt the slowing of the creature to a mere feather of speed. Wings moving before, stilled. Only the waves progressed, the group above, motionless.

—I will tell you of the 47 Ronin of Nausicaa's country, Japan, my Esteemed. Nausicaa is the companion to Kerok, the wisest Alligatorian, my Queen.

A fault occurred in the star dragon, even moving along at a snail's pace.

—No, Brian. Kerok is the wisest SAURIAN, ever. Get priorities straight.

—Apologies, my lady he—

—Tell, tell post-Cro-Magnon teen!

Brian was used to this, thanks to Danillia's distortion of pronouns.

—My Jezzie, just this: The Ronin is translated as 'waves,' waves without a master. In the country of Japan, folks are disciplined, and I'm afraid, hierarchical, too, at least, that's what Nausicaa Lee said. They have different social classes performing different functions. DNA controls us all—only education can counter it.

Jezebellian dismissed this with a whim.

—Nuh. It doesn't. Deoxyribonucleic acid will still be there. Don't think mankind can be perfect. Humans—can't be, hence corruption and all other filth, learn that human ape, if <u>nothing</u> else.

—Anyway, samurai means "the one who serves." I will now cite 'The Ako Incident,' Jezzie. A mere 'picture' of the Ronin only reveals half the story, as you'll see. The power comes from being a minority, and that's where the courage comes from. I'm aware of Larascena's view of "courage," and I think it's not fair to judge humans like dragons.

—I'll deal with the Warlord later. Get on with the story, fool-chimp!

—At your gracious command, my mistress. This takes place around 1700, on Earth, and is true, to my mind, my star-mighty-dragon. This is in feudal Japan. The Samurai class was struggling to keep its proud individuality and the Western groups with their capitalistic bullshit were getting in there and messing it all up. Um, so I understand. The country was a peace for almost 100 years, (setting aside the earthquakes and tsunamis). So, Lord Asano Naganori was chosen by the Shogun, Tokugawa Tsunayoshi to be one of the several daimyo—

—Hold on, what's a daimyo?

—Uh, my Icon, that's a powerful Japanese feudal lord. The "dai" means "large" and the "myo" stands for private land. Can I go on, my mistress?

—Yes, please.

—Alright: So, they were invited to Edo (today, that's Tokyo, the capital city of Japan), to meet and companion, so to speak, the imperial family's envoys. Assigned to assist Lord Asano was the Shogun's highest-ranking member of protocol, Kira Yoshinaka. He was going to show the Lord what to do, with proper court etiquette. They didn't get on well, Jezebellian. Kira wanted to be rewarded, but Lord Asano thought he was only doing his duty. Kira wanted to get paid for his instruction. Kira thought it was disrespectful, and he thought he was superior to Asano.

They didn't use a sparring match, like you would, mistress Jezebellian. Kira embarrassed Asano everywhere, all the time. Just before the main ceremony, the two were talking. Kira called Asano a country piece of dung with no manners. That set Asano off and he went at Kira with his short sword, striking him on the face. This was a great offense, my Queen. After, Lord Asano was questioned. Asano said he should have killed Kira and had no regrets. Not that 'regret' can undo what's coming up. The Shogun heard the story. He was merciful and he selected Hara-kiri.

—What's that?

—My lady, it's like Seppuku.

—What's that?

—Disembowelment, my Jezzie.

—Say what boyfriend? Did they—

—They honorably slit their bellies open with a knife, abdomen gashing and slashing, my mistress.

—Wow; that would be 'death no longer exquisite'?

—Can I go on, my grossed-out lady dragon-star?

—Yeah, do!

—My gracious sovereign, the Shogun said the Lord Asano could commit Hara-kiri, but added to the sentence, the sum of well, $50,000 (or something like that) was added on. When the judgement was announced at Asano's palace, his retainers, now Ronin (without a master) thought about what they should do. They surrendered the palace peacefully. They were in a planning phase, and some kind of revenge seemed certain. Kira knew about the loyalty felt and became paranoid. He was on guard all the time and increased his security. Asano's men just when balling at the local brothels, quite a show. This was evidence as to their disinterest on taking revenge. They are 47 men out of 300 warriors. Two years past, the Kira thought he was safe enough. On December 14, 1702, with snow everywhere, cold night in Edo, the Ronin attacked! Ossie, the head of the Ronin and the fighters fought and then they found Kira in an outhouse. Ossie gave Kira the opportunity to commit Hara-kiri. Kira's response to the request to commit suicide didn't come soon enough for the Ronin, and he was decapitated, head placed in a bucket. The sword used to saw off Kira's head was the same one Asano had used two years prior. The Japanese Emperor said they could all commit Seppuku and they are buried on Sengaku-ji, along with their master. This is the best example of courage, honor and loyalty you'll find if you visit Japan, and I do encourage that *before* we finally leave. They sacrificed for what they *thought* was right. I know, with time, we see truths different than now. With our shortened life span, I think that can be forgiven by the gods, and hopefully you'll get us back to Earth, not arriving at Carcosa and—

—Getting 'political' or, really 'talking shit' yes? The story of the Ronin has unintended consequences. You humans like murder, chaos, debauchery way more than any dragon stars might. That's the secret and one of the reasons why we should *get gone*. The companions are the one thing that can cure us. With our benign (*we think!*) power, we can modify the companions DNA. Thing is, however, where would all the *fun* be?

Jezebellian's wings flew the three humans to their inevitable fate. At-the-sudden, a *shift* on the dragon star's back. Very slight. But there. She looked back in a whirl, like Linda Blair doing the owl-routine in the *Exorcist.*

—Brian Miller you wretched creature! What's going on?

—Lady. We've had...a departure.

—What? Speak you criminal?

—My lady. J. Michael Brower. Jumped.

—From me? He jumped off my back?

—Always amazed at your perceptiveness, Eminence.

Leaving that human obsequiousness 'Gone With the Wind,' the dragon dived down, bullet speed. She was 1,000 feet above Carcosa island

and saw him. In a complex maneuver, she calculated his falling speed and got underneath him.

—Quickly, maggots, get him on board, on my back, beasts of the field!

Marco and Brian reached up. We 'guided him' to a front position, ahead of me, the belletrist splattered forward, semi-conscious.

—Shake the fool awake, turd kickers. Aware now, scribbling bitch? Do that again I'll *skin* you good. I <u>dare</u> you to jump again, shit-on-a-writing-stick. You hear obnoxious scrawler?

—Yes, mistress. I can't help but to hear. Ought to have been different, falling wise.

Jezebellian was swearing to herself. She joined her mastodon fists together and shook them. Jezebellian spoke.

—Whenever <u>that</u> happens again, I will summarily kill the <u>other</u> humans attached to me. And if all three of you take a spill, I'll kill your families hundreds of times over, making you watch. I know something about magic, and you'll live this repeatedly. This involves you AND the families, godsdamn it, I'll be Italian for this instance!

Brian's first time listening to a star dragon threatening a human family. First time for every nightmare. Nevertheless, Carcosa followed hard-upon. Jezebellian felt pissed off.

—This piece of excrement, this writer, know what he did at his little university post-stroke? *Questionable things.* Also, he collected roaches, cockroaches, that he put in a jar with a scientific name, *Blattodea!* And rats, there are a ton of them on this campus. Maybe he's got a Donnie Darko *Cellar Door* <u>collection</u> of them, too?

A tomb-stretched shadow welcomed us to the great, and so sad Carcosa. The sea was a bright blue on arriving, later, something horribly different. Arrested in the sky were two black holes, enshrouded in a fine mist. Suspended there because of an ancient saurian spell. The castle itself, deserted, unlaureled, and putrid. Anyone could see the lamentation, the absolute weeping of the pock-marked half-walls, long bereft of saurian skill and engineering. On the once-noble floors, a sticky and sickly brownish, orange carpet. Everything and anything broken, or near. The blood of the past long spent, suffered howlingly back to a raging sea. Saurians had made the artificial machines, or wretched intelligence that took the place over. It was abandoned, but it was more than that. No wonder you couldn't get a reptilian to reasonably talk of this neglected place. The humans solemnly slid down the dragon star to the squashy carpet at the open-roofed palace. Mankind faces bled white. Any last-hopeful fondness or happy levity ran out the hall with the undead mice chomping at their pitiful feet. Even *Nosferatu* won't attend any night-meetings in this metropolis. The whole thing, a tableau of insanity. It was going back to the sea, in a grindingly slow way. All humans looking at it saw the desiccation, the degeneration, and the environmental-based *deceit* enveloping the city. Even Nature wanted it dead. All the gambrel rooves had fallen almost completely off. The baleful core was visible, you didn't have to 'peal' anything back. It was black, as were most things in the capital. Within an ensanguined mile, it was layers of red, and finally, licking the shore, a shadowy mirk. The beach was everywhere, even the palace had a sheen of water and murky sand. The orange carpet were caked in sea spouge. The towers were falling, spilling back to the gloomy ocean. It was something obscure, liquefied and bloated and full of petrifaction.

—We are going to a once proud city, and a post-fantastic land. Since we are on Lizardania, don't worry, time will pass slowly on Earth, unfortunately. Here, in Carcosa, it is not so. There were dragons here and the Old Ones, too. I don't even know what the Old Ones looked like, those that dwelt in the land of Carcosa. The people here lived under anarchy, and maybe this is what anarchy brings you? As you know, a dragon can never die, unless by violence, or because they just don't feel like going on. You don't realize this about companionship, you dirty humans. It gives the star dragons a reason to live on. You aren't even conscious of the power you have on saurians, especially those that have you as companions. With you, though, this is the end of companionship.

At last, they were before the artificial intelligences of Carcosa, robot-saurians, the 'Andies.' Five sentries moved up behind the leader. The guards' forbear, letting the creature pass, their metal arms extended with some ceremony. The Yellow King himself! Fifteen feet tall, he held a yellow sword, blade down, into the nasty carpet. His wings, draped behind him, on an icky mustard robe. Head down, and a veil covered it, almost completely.

—I'm Jezebellian and I've three humans in need of extreme torture. I've done everything I'm supposed to do. I'm free of Danillia's domination, delivering this garbage to you, my Andies. Brian, Marco and Michael, you will be taken advantage of. You will be exploited, beaten, abused, you'll be an obscenity before these IAs are done. And you are welcome to them, my Yellow King. Kill them slowly, like all the misery and petulance in this unfortunate city. Gods know, I had to keep them in line, torture them sometimes, but I've saved at least a piece of them for you. One, this author here, leapt off me, maybe to save the others? Maybe for himself? Saurian minds can't give a care. I'm going to report back to Danillia. It's all done with me. You human lice? *Don't* <u>farewell</u>, hear?

Marco then said, sadly:

—I'm just a prisoner in a Yellow King's disguise, as we waddle, bye-and-goodbye?

At that, Jezebellian left, snickering to herself at Marco's ephemeral poetry. She flew. A minute past, the three humans, looking at tragedy. The Yellow King moved forward, over the awkward carpet, squishing. Brian, in some solemnity, shuffled to meet the towering IA.

—My lord, I'm the one that's guilty. I will condemn myself but pray these other two of Adam's kind are free?

The Yellow King then laughed hysterically. The veil came off, he shrunk down to his own eight-foot height. It was Kerok! Out came the Black World weapons and, lo and so-beyond, human companions, too. Kerok's sword removed the yellow paint with a solemn wicker, with some noted disgust, the trick done. The Black World weapons did a counter-spell on the saurians, awakening them from Danillia's two-time ruse. It was necessary to get the humans out of Jezebellian's hands, hence waiting for them at Carcosa. Jezebellian could have destroyed all the humans if she suspected anything.

—Let's get out of here, back to Earth! Oh, Brian, your wives took care of the 'Brian Miller' Double, and bigly. I don't think there is anything left of that 'mirror image.' What a laugh it's going to be when Jezebellian briefs Danillia. Talk about getting thrown to the dogs and then getting a chariot to run over your masseter muscle! I don't think Danillia will let Jezebellian survive another sparring match. Saurian madness is not always a deific gift. But you can't have everything?

Then, laughter filled the palace.

The faux-mechanical 'Andies' dispensed with the masks and disguises. The human companions, stood back, enchanted. Littorian, Turinian, Korillia, the two Wysterians, bent down, raising their muscular arms wide, embracing all three humans. Believe me, shiny happy people *filled* the saurians to overload. For two, weight NOTwithstanding!

~~PART THREE~~

Better Few(er)—But Better
by Joan of Arc

"We have listened to it over and over again with great care, and we cannot avoid coming to the conclusion that the words…could have a rather sinister meaning."

—<u>A DAY IN THE LIFE</u>, ON WHY THE *BEETLES* SONG WAS REJECTED BY THE BBC, MAY 23, 1967.

My Dearest Anakimian (Jesus and Mary)!

My companion please, *please* forgive me. Explanation, mine, attend, attend! Did you know that I write *many* letters this way, with my selection of selected Beatitudes? Oh, of that, anon, buy-and-by! Writing is a 'true' weakness of mine. Remember, I couldn't read or write—my helpers did it *for* me! I'm an expert, or maybe just a belletristic apprentice, probably above a sloppy amateur. Some say that I wrote two letters.

Uh! I've a dozen at least!

A rival of mine, (hint-hint, admittedly 400 plus years into <u>our</u> future) an English author Edward Bulwer-Lytton in 1839 said, "The pen is mightier than the sword." Amen to this, Mighty God willing! My French has graduated (some say 'diminished') to English—which has *summa cum laude(d)* into *Universalian*. I prefer '*magna*' it's just my nature! Or my DNA, as Brian likes to say? Of that, too, next pages, please! So hence my letter to you, Anakimian! *Universalian* has a certain mellifluous style, don't you think, my friend? Hopefully you can read my writing. Thesis, Antithesis and then the Synthesis of *Universalian*. My little new-found Trinity, Jesus willing. Of Jesus (<u>controversial</u> in some quarters and of him and Mother Mary) some ((time)) later). And so, in my new, temporary state, in my Mini-Castle (Keep?), I'll be bound, ode to the Black World weapons (doing an amazing, extraordinary, exceptional job, especially on the portcullis, barbicans and machicolations), in the Everglades in Florida (and) in the New World, in America. My letter to you!

Of improved importance, just this: Division of Powers; Executive, Judicial, and Legislative, right? If they fall (or fail), then, something really wrong is happening here. "Doing the right thing will never be the

WRONG thing?" Was it the RIGHT thing to burn me on the pyre? It was the right thing in 1431! I mean, everyone (well, not everybody) agreed. WRONG, though, in 1920 when they made me, *Joan of Arc*, a Saint in the Catholic Church? Excuse me, they can't both be right? Or can they? But then, how many *names* did I have: Jeanne d'Ay de Domremy? Jeanne d'Arc? Jehanne de Vouthon? Jehanne R'omee, Maid of Orleans? The Maiden? Even Jehanne Tars? I'm going to stop this, you've somewhere to fly, my friend! Can, really ALL of them be 'right'?

For me, humans just don't know what a dragon star actually is. They are more (spending much more time in the gym) than any old Velociraptor. It isn't hard to find, at least, for me, The Maid. Genesis, 6:4, said "The Nephilim were on the earth both in those days and afterward, when the sons of God came to the daughters of mankind, who bore children to them. They were the powerful men of old, the famous men." So, as Brian Miller said, the Nephilim, the Fallen Ones, weren't the saurians *I'm* talking about: I do consider them, you reptilians, to be the angels that stayed by God's side, the "good guys." Now, there are bad angels, again, the serpents, that I *do consider* the "fallen ones." I think you might have to refer to <u>Paradise Lost</u>, on that one. We <u>both</u> know who they are. I don't consider the good sons of God to be evil. Maybe that is why the wicked and the heavenly are put side-by-side? Just for an example, I was burned as a witch, you know, by the Catholic Church. With out your saving me, that would be my fate. What is evil today could be good tomorrow? This is just my opinion, ergo my letter to you, my supreme Alligatorian. In 1431 the Church did right, but in 1920 the Church <u>*did right*</u> again? They can't both be true. The ying and the yang, as Sheeta and Jing say? For instance, I would like to 'take a crack' at the 'evil' ones: Genotdelian, Danillia, Jezebellian, Soreidian. I understand some of them are dead. Who really knows, right? Like Littorian says, To Understand All Is To Forgive All? Very true (at least, for NOW it is!). All of you saurians are gods, but, like Commandment the First says, "You shall have no other gods before me"...that isn't to say you SHALL have no 'other' gods: God Almighty is, the MOST high, and I worship Him. Littorian, the Lord of the Lizardanians, believes in the Lord; Larascena, the Warlord of Alligatoria, thinks this is just a laughingstock, she believes in herself only. I understand that Brian Miller has Larascena and Clareina as wives. Oh, that's nothing new: As Socrates said, <u>nothing</u> new under the sun? Didn't Abraham "have" Sarah (his half-sister) Hagar, Keturah, maybe others? Don't they 'share' Ibrahim, and that for the Saracens, or Muslims (that is, 'one who submits' to the Oneness of God or Allah)? True, I've problems with the Muslims, setting up their 'church' about 600 years after the Christians got going, but of that, another time. I'm a teenager, before God, and, with your blood in my body, I will be forever: And I'm a virgin, too. So LONG as it pleases God. Yes, I look on your incredible, massive saurian strength with, well, strong desire. I admit it. Anakimian, I owe you, my life; but it's God that will guide me, and to Him I turn. I've counseled—maybe even encouraged—Him to see it MY way. Uh, er, HARD too, the Holy Spirit praised! On that, I wait. I <u>will</u> be answered too, soon! Our accolated brains crave a little mystery, and that, NOT written down and I'm a truth-teller, praise God. I see 'truth,' in a different way, not like I saw in Domremy. I see it as fluid, like water, truth today, questioned tomorrow? Life is indeed grand, and it is a fluidity (that I can't YET know?). You don't think I'm MOVING at 67,000 miles per second? That space 'smells' like burned stake or gunpowder? I know my artillery, mind, praise God! I know that artillery massed will be more effective on the enemy. I do know, just now, that we, all of us, are moving in space. Changes not stoppable, everything not permanent, but 'Change is!' And I CLAIM the right, the God Almighty Given RIGHT (maybe to women alone?)...to change...my...mind!!! Just stew in my juices a little longer, my friend. Remember: I'm crazy. Or. I'm a Saint and (you should) worship... me? How insane both things are! See me, I laugh (standing, ahem, on a stool) into your darling, equine (and superbly chiseled) countenance, my dragon star companion. Am I the hero in the <u>moment</u>, or only years *after* the fact? Oh, and I've heard you chuckle, to laugh. It's *divinesque*! I'd love to hear it again. Forgive me (once again) of my youth—but I'll <u>always</u> have my 'teenagerhood,' once, now, and forever and a day, again, praise Mary! Some wonder if I live everlastingly in a sincere sin—for now, I know it <u>isn't</u>. But. Change! (is!). Nothing permanent. And that scares me, really. Is my Love for God…permanent? Anti-love for the Devil Not Permanent? What is Lasting (forever?). As you know, 'contradiction,' is spelled that way in French, too. You saurians have SOLVED contradiction for me. *For now.*

Yes, as humans, we're all wild animals, with <u>this</u> difference. At times, we are *not*, we are just 'becoming' wild animals with a meticulous conscience. We've a certain *naivete*. Thank God for the French Language, eh? The joy of life hasn't (quite) gotten away from me as a teenager. Sure, we've the strength, the willingness (if <u>properly</u> convinced), the youthful power, and the proper, sometimes boundless, joy to carry it forward. See, I've never known 'adulthood.' By your blood, I hope never to, too! Only violence can bring me low. With my Five Black World Weapons. Well… I'm unstoppable? Every-human can be…corrupt. The Maid of Orleans? Ah, I remember those times, carrying my banner. It's time to leave this Earth, God-only-willing.

Let me turn to the pile of books I've in front of my face, about companions and star dragons! The first, only a very few have read it (or, by now, have SUFFERED through it!) <u>Brian Miller & the Twins of Triton</u>. Dragons and teenagers can't appeal to everyone. This book was authored by Katrina and Brian Miller, and by Kat's Dad, too! High school machinations are sorta new to me, by the Holy Ghost, it's true. These drugs these kids had access to lord of mercy all things of the Devil! Gangs and the strictions of capitalism, yikes. The introduction of Leah Starblue and Joe Triassic as shapeshifters is very interesting to me personally. Maybe just to show my sad naiveite. I guess my eccentricity was overwhelming to peasants, er, *everywo/man*. And teenagers and little kids. I was under God's will, maybe I wasn't myself? The idea that one of my own 'visions' might have been really a perception of shapeshifting saurians, I do have to consider. I asked you about this, my companion Anakimian. I know about Enoch and what he saw. These 'Radiant Ones' maybe these were the 'good' serpents? I know about the Eastern and Western views of these dragons. Most are good, some bad. The Seraph has six fiery wings. Did I see this angel? Or was it just 'visions'? I don't mean to tell you what you already know, my lord. Even your name "Anakimian" means 'giant,' the offspring of fallen angels and mortal women. And I don't think you're a Nephilim, either. True, I don't know how the Alligatorian, Crocodilian, Lizardanian or Wysterian history interacts here. I'm just a simple teen, gratefulness to the Lord. I'm for leaving the Earth. It's not a defeat. Having dragon spirits on Earth is not good for humanity.

Turning (around) back to the 'non-novels,' the spirit of Katrina and Brian, inspires me. I do know what the 'liaisons hinted at' off and on. Yes, I know what it is to have 'compassion' as a teenager. I don't think I can forgive it, it's just part of this life, my friend! Holy Ghost and the debates you guys had at the Pentagon (that atrocious war machine), in Israel, and that garbage heap in the Philippines, that's some powerful stuff. What happens in the next books, things are quite turned around, Book Two, <u>Brian Miller & the Young Star Dragons</u>, that's a (twisted) turn I didn't expect. And the Third Book, <u>Brian Miller & the Alien Shore</u>, the very longest, all kinds of things are developed, and the love that no one knows, it's all there, the love between the saurians and the companions. Here's the thing: If God said it's alright, who are we to question? I'm not the ONLY one who hears the Lord.

Danillia really frightens me. Jezebellian, too. All this, only a precious few months elapsed, incredible, unbelievable! This book is full of adventures, Katrina telling it to a 'T'—that's another thing: Did God and

Jesus create all of them? That only strengthens my conviction in the Lord. I appreciate that I'm JUST going through this and that you are kind of patient with me, my saurian friend.

I'm writing this missive in my Mini-Castle. The Black World weapons are a Godsend. I picked out my weapons on the Dark Planet and that's a joy to tell too! Two knives, two hatchets, and a Black World sword. I love them all. Like as with you, bands of steel surround my passion. Are these weapons send by angels? Or Jesus? I remember Matthew 10:34, I came not to send peace but a sword. Now, I can't read Hebrew or Yiddish—yet! And I endorse the One Right of Women: To CHANGE her mind. No matter the age; no matter what. I have seen the anarchist vision and know these views are only safe for saurians, not for humans to know.

Getting back to Book One, Kat and Brian have my greatest faith and respect. That Brian gave up on power, to pass this all to *the Maid*, is made clear in Book Four and Five. Now Brian is a bit 'crafty' but I refuse to think of him as cruel. It's like, for instance, "La Hire" ('knave of hearts') or formally Etienne de Vignolles. Not going to 'equate' Brian with La Hire. However. They do know the way to get 'things' done in a round-about way. I'm aware of what La Hire did, looking back on my history. Of course, I had nothing to do with it. At Patay, France, he won a great battle. All generals go through this—you can't 'control' them. I don't want to. I want them to obey God. As you know, I'm very plain. Brian despite his craftiness, has a romance with Lara and Clare. Is that not, in a way, the same crime as La Hire? I judge people for what they are. Not who I want them to be. You've lived a long, long time, Anakimian. Can someone bring me things that are 'untoward' in your own history? I judge based on ACTS not 'imagination' or such thingy-things. I love you. You *saved* me. I saw it. I'm a simple teen. A peasant, a yeo*women*. And I'm looking forward to being judged by God. I'm a virgin; I love being with you. That will last <u>as long as God wants</u>. And no longer. Believe me on that. With all this gorgeous dragon blood I'm drinking, well, I can *barely* wait!

I can't review all of Brian's books at the moment. I just saw you fly down to my Mini-Castle entrance. What the Black World weapons have done to the Everglades is just storybook, it's pristine. I'm sure you'll be waited on by my well-wishers. A few other things, though, about these books. I've talked to Brian about these goings-on, and he says <u>Brian Miller Supplemental</u> is the best book. That's him falling in love with Lara. Well, didn't *something* like that happen in Romeo and Juliet? I've consumed that much of the classics. As humans, we've got to change our minds, about everything! Things can be true, even our principles, our truths, our rights. But CHANGE is! As teens, they could DO everything adults can do. Right, my companion? The 1% run everything and anything in this country, really, the world. Any plain person can see this. Matthew 19:24 "it is easier for a camel to go through the eye of a needle than for a rich person to enter the Kingdom of God." So, I think 'what is going on' between teenagers and star dragons, given time, is well...kinda natural.

I think, leaving Earth, that we're on the cusp of 'founding' it again? Planets in the Goldilocks Zone or a Sunflower Familial, or a Butterfly Partition already found by the Wysterian, Teresian? And *Tiperia*, Littorian's girlfriend, can get millions, billions of our 'water-based bodies' to future-Earth in a day (or two) and a night? For my Catholicism, I think existence is just another form of punishment. *Tiperia* could prove me wrong, though. Right to *Change my Mind*. I might invoke it.

Ah, this letter just goes on, doesn't it? Editors, just try to stricture my radical words. Yes, I understand hierarchy. And I can see why dragon stars reject it. As a revolutionary, I feel like a turnip: Conservative on the inside (white) red on the outside. I see on my grand desk a fledging story by Brian Miller. *Top Horror at the Reamsville Station*. That doesn't have much appeal to me. As a general, I've seen more blood and...if only I could forget! I thought that adventures were without violence. It's not. With you there, Anakimian, then I can rest assured.

Wait, just wait my companion, delay awhile, delay! Before making a judgment on all humanity, consider my 600-year resurrection? I'm not a stranger to you, Anakimian. Like Marco said, "I'm no stranger. I'm Marco!" Oh, and of course, letter-writing is 'my Bae'. See? Up with today's slang, like Brian Miller says, "Ain't it cool?" Anon, adventures to keep you reading, a letter by me, Joan of Arc? Oh, poo, read along, just in spite of me. To counter all that pessimism, mentioned at the outset of my letter to you, I propose to banish all that skepticism to the fly-splatted regents ruled by Lucifer. Taking over the Thirty Companions, that Brian Miller dutifully gave me, I've this to say to all of them: God be praised! I'm going for good cheer! Justice with ever-living mercy! Be a compassion to humanity, and great and unmistakable faith and love in the Lord, and the Son of the Lord. And of the Daughters of the Lord, too. That much I've learned through my Faith and Hope! And listen, my saurian Anakimian—I am learning, and will learn still. Of all the people in THE WORLD to save? I've got to make you think you made the right choice. Not until you learn to weep for the afterimage, for the post-innocence. I've an idea, however, like plastic, every teenager can learn new notions. Of course, we have skeptics, doubters, among companions and my alien sisters and brothers. There are good Companions. And bad. There are good Dragon Stars. And ones needing a little help. I'm for helping where I can and when I can. Can I see Good and Evil?

I hope you don't feel dragooned (ahem) into reading all this, my compassionate star dragon. It's good to talk (I mean to write), right? Differences in opinions aren't differences over principles. I'm principled, but change IS! With dragon stars, and the companions, I've found, well, stuff is more complicated, an antithesis to my humble simplicity. Even principles, like truth, are fluid over time. What is truth now, questionable tomorrow. A limited life span needs to hold on to things, like Catholics can.

The truth shall out? The truth is *'a becoming,'* like water. Star dragon 'truth' on science has revealed that to me. <u>For now</u>. And for you, we can't stay on Earth. Suffer me to go to Teresian, the Wysterian, and appeal to her, for all humanity? Still, I wish to go with you Anakimian and be a kindly General to the 30, don't you think?

However. Maybe, *just maybe,* we shouldn't leave as soon as we otherwise might? Like Littorian, the Lord of the Lizardanians said once, 'on the other hand...I think I'll stay...for a day'...or so?

With All My Gargantuan Pre-Love,

Printed in the United States
by Baker & Taylor Publisher Services

Printed in the United States
by Baker & Taylor Publisher Services